St. Basil

D1523230

By

Carl Vincent

Prologue

I'm writing this account because I enjoy it. This is a purely hedonistic exercise. I'm not trying to make money or enlighten myself or anyone else. It's pleasurable for me to write. There are a ton of things that are also pleasurable for me, but most of those things either cause cancer or incarceration. Writing causes neither. Unless you're in China.

I'm sharing it because Basil suggested it. He said there were a couple of parts that made him smile. I wouldn't mind it if I made someone smile. I've made enough people cry over the years, so maybe I can balance that out a little. But mainly I'm sharing it because Basil said to. As I look back on my life, I think it would have been less complicated had I followed suggestions. No regrets, though. No use in that. Even if I had a DeLorean I'd wreck it before I got it up to 88mph. With that reference, now you know I'm a Boomer. Old and white. It hasn't been our finest year.

So who am I? Most books have an "About the Author" section, so I guess this is that. Here's everything you need to know about me: When I was a child, if you were to ask me the "super power" question (If you could have one super power...) I would have said

Speed of Light or maybe Superhuman Strength. When I became an adolescent and started to discover girls, my answer would have been Invisibility. That would have been fun! As an adult I would have chosen Seeing Into the Future, mainly for lottery purposes. As an older adult, if I could choose any super power, I would now choose Sleep on Command. So that's pretty much my whole life story in a paragraph.

Whether the events described herein are true or not would depend completely on your perspective. From my point of view, this is exactly how the events unfolded.

I've kept some names the same, but changed others. If you were a part of this story but you're not in here, one of two things is true. Either you have been nothing but an absolute joy to me or you weren't worth the ink.

Finally, I am alive to share this account only because of the love and care of three people. They are of the sort who would rather not be named in a book. But they know who they are. They are also aware that, on the days when I am glad to be alive, I am grateful for them. And on the days when I'm disappointed to wake up, I blame them. Most days they have my deep gratitude.

1.

I made the short walk into town, wearing the same faded dickies I had on yesterday, but with a fresh t-shirt. I'll re-wear pants, but not shirts. I go in through the back of the diner, the smell of yesterday's meals fill the air from the dumpster. Time has not been good to them. In through the back door, clock in, and start my shift. I love my job! I make dirty plates clean. I do that for 8 hours without so much as a word to anyone. I am, apart from my task, unimportant. I only get questions about plates and utensils. The questions don't even require an answer. Are we out of plates? Do you have spoons? The questions just require fulfillment. Eight hours goes by exceedingly fast.

I clock out and pick through a few items that didn't make the cut for the day, bag it up and head home. I walk through the door, turn on the light, and I'm greeted with the most glorious sight. Every single thing is exactly where I left it. Only Basil is there to greet me. And not because I matter, but because I bring dinner with me. Basil gets some chicken and milk. I get a burger and some fries. We eat together in the light of the old TV, never saying a word. Matlock doesn't need any commentary. I am at peace, watching a cat watch me as I watch a guy who was a better sheriff than an attorney. The universe is expanding at the speed of light. Millions of people are engaged in Very Important Things, and I am finally as invisible as I have always wanted to be my whole life. All of these years. All of that education. All of that procreation. The striving and the working and the grunting and the fucking and the screaming and the bleeding have all come down to this: I am only known if a plate is dirty or if Basil needs to eat. If I could have known how happy this makes me, I could have saved myself and a lot of people a significant amount of heartache.

As I drift off to sleep, I wonder, if I pass in the night, how many days before Basil decides to see me as a source of nutrition instead of the provider of it? And will he start and the head or the feet? I look it up, and cats will wait about a day. Dogs, a little longer. Dog people that read that will assume it's because the dog has compassion for its owner. More likely, the dog is just a little slower to figure it out.

2.

I enjoy my own company these days. And I have an active imagination, which saves money on entertainment expenses. I've always had an active imagination, but I've not always enjoyed my own company. I have spent many years, most of my adult life, trying to be acceptable to the person in front of me. In addition to being exhausting and confusing, it is the death sentence to identity. You never know who you are. So when you're alone, you're with a stranger. Plus, if you're trying to make everybody happy, you are devoid of personal ambition. I have certainly earned the place I am in. It's modest. Humble. OK, it's Spartan. You could literally put everything I own in the back of someone else's car. You could put it in mine if I had one. I sold mine as soon as I got out here. The feet still work just fine.

3.

Basil is important to me. Not in the same way a cat lady loves her cats. Or the same way I see people develop some kind of strange attachment to their pets. I'm under no illusions. Basil and I have a symbiotic relationship. We meet each other's needs, and for that, we have respect for one another. That's as far as it goes. Here's the strange part. Basil understands what I say. And I understand him. We have been together long enough that I can tell when he rolls his eyes at my jokes or when he's pissed because the water isn't fresh enough. I can even tell when he swears. "Dammit" is his most common swear. But "Motherfucker" is his most prolific. Samuel Jackson would be proud. Basil usually reserves "Motherfucker" for the times when he forgets about the window and a bird shows up right outside. In an instant, with obviously cat like reflexes, Basil goes from a near feathered orgasm to remembering the physics of glass. It's an instant double disappointment. The only human analogy I can think of at the moment is this: You go into the gas station and you buy a scratch off lottery ticket. You take it home, because you're feeling kind of lucky and you're not one for public displays. You scratch it off and you have a winner! You're dancing around to the idea that you just won a thousand dollars and in your excitement you slip on the rug and you land on the floor, where a fork left on the floor proceeds to pierce your taint. And as you're writhing in pain, you look over at the lottery ticket and you see you were one number off. Motherfucker. That's how Basil feels when he smacks against the glass.

I'll admit, having a cat that talks to me took some getting used to. Basil and I just accept it. Who would you tell, really? After a couple of days it seemed pretty normal to me.

He and I met at my apartment complex a few months back. I was coming home from work one evening and there he was, just hanging out by my door. He wasn't jumpy like some of the dumpster cats I've been around. He wasn't purring or meowing like he wanted anything. In fact, it didn't look like he needed anything at all. He was just there. So we got to know each other over the next few days. Just simple greetings. Then one night I had brought some fish home from the diner. I asked him if he'd like to come in and eat dinner with me. He said, "Sure." And I didn't think it too odd that he answered me. So that's how we met.

Basil has picked up another expression lately. First, you should know Basil was born in Elko, Nevada, where he currently resides. Basil has not been outside of Elko his entire life. Furthermore, while I have spent most of my years NOT in Elko, Nevada, now that I'm here I'm not leaving. Neither Basil nor I have any need for a passport.

That being said, Basil's new phrase is a kind of British slang. He says, "Oi!" Imagine if Russell Brand were a cat. Now imagine your cat likes to take a lot of chemicals for pleasure. And you just took your cat's chemicals away and flushed them down the toilet. Now you can hear how Basil says, "Oi!" Except Basil only uses this expression when I short him at dinner. Or if I spill a little water by his bowl. He gets a cup for lunch and a cup for dinner and he'll have nothing and like it for breakfast. Well, if I give him a little less than a cup for dinner, that's when I get the "Oi." I have no idea where he picked that up. I don't even watch the BBC. We're a rabbit ear family. It could be from that one time we watched "Snatch" together. I loved it, but Basil had a strong negative reaction to Brick Top. I thought Alan Ford was a genius. Agree to disagree.

Most nights are pretty uneventful. A little food, a little entertainment. Some light conversation, then off to bed. What's not to like? I mentioned before that Basil and I have a symbiotic relationship and I told you what I do for him. What he does for me is a little more in the clouds. I obviously don't need Basil to fix my dinner or pay the rent. Basil does two things for me, both of which I need. First, he stays. I give him plenty of opportunities with doors and windows. And he could just ask. But he chooses to stay with me. And the second, and most important, thing is this: He is not fundamentally disappointed in me. Now there's no need for you to feel sorry for me. I have earned almost all of the disappointment I've experienced in life. But I have felt, for most of my life, that I am simply not enough. I can't shake it. I've tried therapy (briefly), alcohol (not briefly) and all manner of distractions. It's not in focus. I'm not certain what would be different if I were enough. I'm not sure how people would treat me different and I'm not sure how I would be different. But I'm enough for Basil. Even when I short his dinner or laugh at him running into a window. I'm enough. So they're connected, right? He stays because I'm enough. My two favorite qualities about Basil: He is not greedy and his standards are low. We're perfect for each other.

4.

When I was younger I had the thought, "Nobody cares about me" and it made me sad. That same thought gives me freedom today. Sitting here, on this spinning ball, one of nine spheres (I realize its counter transference, but it seriously pissed me off when Pluto got the ax, so in solidarity for all the dismissed, there are 9 planets), one of 500 solar systems (and growing), and one of two trillion galaxies. One of Two Trillion Galaxies!!! Motherfucker! How could anything matter??? Seriously? Your aunt made an insensitive comment on your Facebook? He left you on Read? Really???? Oi!!! Nothing matters. I think I remember this quote from Groundhog Day: "What if there's no tomorrow? There wasn't one today!!"

When I was younger I wanted to matter. To a woman. To Humanity. To God. The "matter" I wanted to make was, I wanted to make your life better. Sounds altruistic, doesn't it? Sounds like I'm a nice guy, right? If you've met me, you know this just simply isn't true. Yeah, I do some nice things. I try to avoid doing the really terrible things. But the reason I wanted to matter was more about me than it was about you. I wanted to matter so that I would matter. If I made your world better, if I walked you closer to God, if I helped quell the demons in your mind, if I helped you slay the beast, well, then, I must have value. I have never had, don't have, and never will have, what they describe as "ego strength." My ego has always been wrapped up in my reflection when I look at you. I've worked on that enough that it doesn't cripple me. And I've made my world smaller and reduced my emotional footprint enough. Needless to say, nobody has ever accused me of being an Influencer.

I overheard a couple of customers the other day. I only caught part of the discussion. I heard one say to the other, "I'm just trying to stay relevant." What the even heck? That's an old phrase (attributed to Miranda Sings) a daughter of mine used to say, which is, by the way, not relevant but still funny to me.

First, let's deal with the presumption: To want to "stay" relevant is to assume that one is currently relevant. And how do you come around to that conclusion? Is there a RQ? A Relevance Quotient? Some sort of test I can take? Or is it based on how many people "like" what I create? What if I make a 60 second video with my bottom titty showing? I think the correct term is "underboob," but I like "bottom titty." Yes, I have a bottom titty. I'm a cis male named Carl. I've got a penis and everything. But due to some questionable life choices there is a defined area of my body that could be termed as such. Anyway, nobody wants to see my bottom titty. Basil makes me wear a shirt around the house for that very reason. I came out of the shower once shirtless and Basil popped out a hairball on command. Right at my feet. Basil said, "I swear to fucking Garfield if I see that sweaty mass again I'll wait 'til you're asleep and I'll shit right in your belly button and we both know you won't find it for a week." I get dressed in the bathroom now.

So I guess once you attain Relevance, then comes the task of keeping it? And how do you do that? You know what's relevant? A vaccine. Harry Styles is relevant. But phrases and fashion, that's not relevant. That's kinda "sus" to me. "SUS" is short for suspicious. I learned it the other day at the diner. What's really suspicious is when I hear people trying to come up with a sentence that contains the word "suspicion" so they can be casual about the use of "sus." That's REALLY sus! And I just got another eye roll from Basil.

Basil seemed to indicate he was getting a little tired of our old re-runs on TV, so for a few nights we watched Jimmy Fallon on an old iPad I picked up at the pawn shop. I guess he's relevant. He's funny, and he seems nice, unlike Ellen. Ellen wishes she was nice, and genuinely tries to be nice. Watch her on her game show sometime. Watch her face when a contestant falls. Look at the joy on her face when that happens. She can't help it and I wish people would leave her alone. You're either nice, not nice and wish you were (which makes you niceish), or you're just a son of a bitch. Jimmy is nice.

Ellen isn't really nice but tries hard to be. And we all know the son of a bitch.

So Basil and I are watching Jimmy make jokes about what's happening now. So he's current (is that relevant? I guess they're synonymous). And then, out of nowhere, Basil turns to me and says, "Why can't you be more like Jimmy?"

Well, I admit, I'm moderately offended. Only moderately because I realize the observation has come from someone who licks his own asshole.
"What do you mean, 'more like Jimmy?'"

Basil said, "Well he just looks nice. He probably smells nice. I bet he doesn't even have toe jam."

Well, he has me there.

Maybe being relevant means being talked about. If that's the case you can have it. I've been a topic of conversation before and I can tell you it was not pleasant for me. I even hate getting gifts. All my life I've told people not to make a big deal out of my birthday. And everybody thinks I'm just being modest. I REALLY JUST DON'T WANT THE ATTENTION! So where does that come from? Is that tied to my lack of self-worth? Who knows. I know last year when Basil and I shared a cupcake I brought home from the diner (I celebrate his birthday on mine because he doesn't remember his date) it was one of the best birthdays I can recall.

I wonder if relevance and happiness are mutually exclusive. You want to know who is happy? Garnett Simpson is happy. Do you know Garnett? You don't, do you. You might know someone by that name, although it's doubtful. But I guarantee you don't know Garnett. He's the happiest guy I know. He lives out in the desert in a little shack, comes into town about once a month. You can see it in his eyes. A deep contentment with his pace and position. I also guarantee if you did know him he would be less happy than he is right now. Don't take that as an insult, just a fact. People bring problems. Is he relevant? Depends on how you measure it.

He pronounces his name in a way that would rhyme with "darn it." Just so you know. I saw him last month and I said, "Garnett, do you ever plan on getting a cell phone?"

He said, "Now why would I sell my phone? Who would buy it? It's not even hooked up to nothin'."

That is what we might call a "coping strategy." He pretends to not hear you so you have to repeat yourself and spend twice the energy to talk to him, making you think twice about it next time.

I told Basil about Garnett selling his phone and he said, "You know he regrets talking to you, right? Sometimes people regret talking to you."

5.

Since we're talking a lot about Basil let me give you a visual. Basil is a short haired cat, thin, with gray and white fur. I don't understand the different kinds of cats, so Basil is a regular cat. I know there are long hair cats, and Basil isn't one of those. I've also seen pictures of hairless cats, and I'm more inclined to donate money to their cause than for the starving kids in Africa. I can't imagine what must go through the mind of hairless cat. I haven't spent much time on it, but a hairless cat must certainly be kept away from mirrors. Do regular hair cats feel embarrassed for the hairless cat? I think the Germans called it Fremdschämen. Something like vicarious embarrassment? Like when you see a person with their fly down, you feel bad for them. To my knowledge, Basil has never seen a hairless cat. I think I'll show him a picture tonight.

So is there some class order among cats based on hair length? I've never owned a long hair cat, but I suspect they might be more indifferent or aloof than a regular cat. Maybe I think that because they must groom more, just to keep up.

Unlike me, Basil has excellent ego strength. Basil knows he is a cat. He knows there are other cats. And he knows I am not a cat. So he's pretty self-aware. But there is not a molecule in him that wants to be anything different than what he is. Basil has never experienced FOMO in his life (unless you count the days that a window prevents him from bagging a bird). Basil doesn't want to be a long hair or a hairless cat.

Basil and I watched Tiger King together at the beginning of the pandemic. We sat silently though every episode and never said a word to each other. We were both amused, but didn't feel the need to talk about it. If you don't know how pure that is then I'm not sure we can still be friends. Anyway, we sat through the whole series and Basil got to see all manner of what they call Big Cats. Regal, powerful, exotic. Spots, Manes, teeth as big as bananas.

While the end credits were rolling, all he said was, "You know that bitch killed her husband right?"

"You think so?" I said.

"Yeah, and not only that, he had it coming. Just look at the guy. You see how close his eyes are together? Man, that guy ain't right. Good for her. And I'll give you one more thing to think about: How do you think her next lover is going to treat her? He better come correct. She might be the joke to society, but whoever is shacking up with her is going to treat her right!"

I try not to smile when Basil talks tough like that. I'm not sure where he picked the phrase, "better come correct." Maybe he doesn't stay home when I leave? Maybe that movie, "Secret Life of Pets" was a documentary.

I remembered I intended to show Basil a picture of a hairless cat! I think I saw one in a magazine at the barbershop so I stopped the next day and asked Slick (a nickname, I assume) if I could take the page home. Slick asked what for. I lied, "I want to send it to my nephew back east." I don't have a nephew back East, but I can't very well tell someone, even Slick, that I want to show it to my cat.

So I showed Basil the picture after dinner. He looked at it without expression. Cocked his head to the side and looked some more. He was silent for maybe two minutes. Then said, "Hmmm. No hairballs. I'm down."

Basil has never, to my knowledge, had the pleasure of female company. Nor does he have the necessary equipment for such a venture. But I swear he kind of had a sexy voice when he said that. I imagined my voice if Diane Lane asked me to rub her calves after a long day on the set where she did NOT have sex with Richard Gere. Same thing, minus the hairballs.

6.

I'll keep my self-description brief. I could let you use your imagination, but that would be too risky. Basically, I look exactly like if Russell Brand and Justin Bieber had a baby. Except I'm 5'9", stocky, fair skinned (and poorly complected) of Welsh decent, and I shave my head. So actually, more like Shrek on a good day.

7.

I've got family, but I'm in a relational self-quarantine.
For the past few years, really. Whatever reputation I
might have I'm certain that I earned it. I read a story
the other day about a guy who was freed after 18 years
in prison. Turns out, they got the wrong guy. They
interviewed him the next day when they released him
and asked him, "Are you bitter?" If that had been me
I'd be back in prison that night for reporter assault. He
lied his ass off. "I'm just happy to be here, I'm not
bitter at all!" I'm actually bitter about it. When you get
on the wrong side of the law they treat you different. If
you're accused you lose some of your rights and all of
your considerations. Like basic considerations such as
manners. My actions got me there, no sugar coating
that. I'm bitter about the guy getting 18 years because
it's another page in the Life Isn't Fair book.

Another guy I read about in the 1800's went to jail for wearing a beard (at a time when facial hair was frowned upon). That guy was a badass. Refused to pay the $10 fine. I think he stayed locked up for the better part of a year. Maybe more. Basil's over in the corner, minding his own business, giving himself a bath. He mumbles under his breath, "A motherfuckin' beard."

I really like living with Basil.

I'm relationally quarantined for one reason really. Over the course of my life I have interacted with thousands of people. I have helped some and I have hurt some. And I usually can't tell when I meet you which one that will be. So what's the score? I don't know. I'd say I helped more than I hurt, but I couldn't be sure about that. I bet I've hurt a lot of people and don't even know about it. Some people have had it coming. I'm glad I hurt them. When I think about those times I'm proud of the pain. But others didn't deserve it. Nobody is the villain of their own story. Nobody thinks they're the bad guy. The human mind's ability to construct functional fictions and reframe reality is not to be underestimated. So I don't think I'm the bad guy in my story, but I might very well be. There's a dozen or so people that would tell you I am the villain.

I think about Kelly sometimes, my college roommate. One day he casually introduces me to nicotine. I had smoked before, but only occasionally. This day was different. That day started a 30 year habit that only God himself was able to break in me. I wonder if Kelly ever thinks about that. I can't imagine any reason why it might have crossed his mind. I wouldn't expect it to.

But it had a profound impact on my life just the same. I assume God broke that habit in me, because I sure didn't have the strength. But I also know people go to jail who don't deserve it and kids get cancer. So I'm not fully convinced God did that. It feels like he did though. And if he did, then I know it was a gift, because there are some rotten, evil parts in me.

The miracle, given the size of this place, is that we feel or sense a creator at all. I also think it's funny that we use male pronouns for God. Actually, it's kind of funny that we use any name at all. I liked it when the Jews made God's name without vowels so it couldn't even be said. They were onto something. Basil calls God "Bastet." Why, I don't know. Actually, I don't want to know. A being's relationship to their creator is such a personal thing. Maybe that's where we messed up. The creator of two trillion galaxies surely can't be understood by the creation? Or named? The canvas doesn't name the piece. The artist does.

In North America religion seems to be on the decline. 5% of churches are closing annually, and the pandemic we're in is likely to double that number. I've tried churches before and I never got anywhere with it. I really did give it a go. But the ones I tried ended up being just clubs. I wasn't looking for a club. I was looking for existential resolve. I have only ever found that in music, nature, and animals. I grew up thinking taking God's name in vain meant using the name "God" casually. Like in a curse. As an adult, I've learned that the commandment is broken when we attribute things to God that are actually not of God. So, plagiarism.

Basil's take was "that motherfucker Kenneth Copeland telling people God wanted him to have a fucking jet is what the fucking fourth commandment is about."

But there's thousands of people that are lined up to eat up the shit he spews out and they'll swear it smells like a rose. I wonder if modern medicine has gotten too good. I heard for years that God was going to send a plague to rid the earth of the unfaithful. And here we are in the middle of a pandemic that is taking hundreds of thousands of lives, and the anti-mask crowd and the church folk are one in the same. By the way, I'm talking about the evangelical white church. The black church is on the right side of history on this thing. Most of the white church is a bunch of pro-Trump (Basil calls him Dorito Mussolini), anti-mask, racist, homophobic, transphobic, anti vax, flat earth idiots who couldn't find their ass with a search warrant. See why I don't play well with others?

So yes, God is important to me. But the brick and mortar church isn't. I remember trying one back East. It was growing like wildfire! People were coming in droves! The funny part was the pastor was really a dick. And not just a little bit. He was a real asshole. He passed it off as being "authentic" and everybody thought that was wonderful. He wasn't Jimmy or Ellen.

Basil and I are fans of God, but we don't think God is in control around here. You'd really have to be an idiot to look around and think that any intelligent, benevolent being is conducting this shit orchestra. But we sure think that nature is beautiful. Basil watches from the window and I take every chance I can to get out in it. Clearly, it is designed by a creative, loving, benevolent, Supreme Being.

Some have taken exception with my coarse language, saying that God is unhappy with it. But if you think my use of the word "fuck" is obscene and you don't think telling gay people that they're broken is obscene then we seriously can't be friends.

Speaking of friendship tests, here's another one. I read a headline the other day: "Irish dwarf accused of posing as a leprechaun to extort sex from 26 women in exchange for a pot of gold."

Not only is that funny, I think Jesus would laugh at that too. So would Irish dwarfs. I actually know an Irish dwarf and he about pissed his pants when I read it for him. When he quit laughing, I took the opportunity for him to educate me about proper terms. He said "midget" is offensive, and most people with dwarfism prefer "little people" or "dwarf." But only if stature is a part of the conversation. Otherwise, he said he just prefers people to use his name.

8.

I miss who I thought my mother was.

9.

The French word for boredom and irritation is Ennui. But the root suggests it is annoyance after indulgence.

Basil and I had a fight today. I gave him his dinner and he seemed more annoyed than usual at my portion control. He finally said (in his best Clint Eastwood voice), "What say we live a little?"

Fine. So I'm the bad guy. Mr. Portion Control over here. Dr. Funkiller (an actual name given to me by someone I tried to help once when I was still trying to help people). Actually, can I have a word with you for a moment? It'll only take a second.

When I used to tell others about the nickname, Dr. Funkiller, I would do so in a jovial manner. An amusing anecdote. But actually, fuck that guy. I didn't knock on his door and tell him he couldn't take drugs. His wife dragged him to me because he was destroying his family. His "fun" wasn't fun for anyone else but him. So I'm taking your toys away? The nickname belonged to him, not me. Just so we're straight, I'm a lot of fun. Ok, let me get back to the dinner fight.

"Here, let's see what you can do with this!" I brought two leftover chicken breasts out of the fridge and sat them down with a big bowl of milk. Basil hasn't been this happy since Iams came out with a pinup calendar. I had to look at Miss March's hairy ass for three months straight. So Basil dug in. It looked like a crime scene. He finished every bite. I got him more food from the fridge, and then topped it off with a little ice cream. Basil finished all of that too. He and I are so much alike. When he finished he just kind of listed off to the side and fell down with a thud. We just looked at each other for a few minutes. He didn't say anything; he didn't have to. He didn't feel the way he thought he would feel after he finished that meal. He thought he would feel content and happy. Instead, you could see it in his eyes: regret.

Then blame: "Why'd you let me eat all of this...?" He got up suddenly and waddled over to the side of the couch and threw up half a chicken breast and at least a tit's worth of milk. Maybe two.

I have no judgement for him. None. I'm watching a home movie of my own life. See. Taste. Eat. Gorge. Regret. Repeat. I never could stop halfway through that process. As I was thinking about that Basil started nibbling on what he had just expelled moments earlier. Now it's complete. We're identical twins. Except I can't lick my own asshole. And even if I could, I wouldn't. The difference between Basil and me is that I'll not allow Basil to do this again, and I have autonomy. I get to decide what portions I have of what and when. Whoever thought that was a good idea was a fucking moron.

10.

I'm reading (again) John Steinbeck's East of Eden. Here's a gem: "In uncertainty I am certain that underneath their topmost layers of frailty men want to be good and want to be loved. Indeed, most of their vices are attempted short cuts to love. When a man comes to die, no matter what his talents and influence and genius, if he dies unloved his life must be a failure to him and his dying a cold horror. It seems to me that if you or I must choose between two courses of thought or action, we should remember our dying and try so to live that our death brings no pleasure to the world."

My death will actually bring pleasure to some. But I will not be leaving the earth unloved either. But what he said about vices really stuck with me. Short cuts to love. My vices were an attempt to find satiety. Like Basil, they never did. But Steinbeck said that underneath our topsoil we want to be good and we want to be loved. I guess I have wanted those things before in my life. I would say, today, I am loved. I would also say, today, I have been fairly good. I don't know exactly how to define that one. What does that even mean? Good. I've been to a lot of funerals (a friend just died today) and I've heard, "He was a good man. She was a good woman. He was a good dog."

Basil is actually a good cat. Yeah, he's surly. He says "fuck," a lot. He's rude sometimes and he also thinks about himself first. But he's not trying to hurt anyone. And I don't have to guess what's on his mind. Not that he feels compelled to "tell it like it is." But he's congruent. He's not a closet Republican. He thinks Ted Cruz is Cosplay Wolverine and he'll tell you about it. To describe someone as "good" is so vague. Basil laughs when someone slips on the ice. Out loud. He points his furry paw at them and cackles wildly. But he doesn't pretend not to laugh.

I once knew a cat named Scooter. Before I met Basil I would have said, "I had a cat named Scooter." But Basil has enlightened me on ownership. Anyway, Scooter was a polite cat. He would do what he was told. If you scolded him, he looked contrite. When he was around you he would be affectionate and grateful. An all-around good being. But he would absolutely jump on the counter and start eating food if it was left out. And he would absolutely go throw up that food on the carpet if he thought no one was looking. And he would most definitely beat the living shit out of his step brother, Tybee, as long as no humans were around to see it.

Maybe we have confused polite and good? Basil isn't polite. He would absolutely, given the chance, shit in the sand box of the neighbor kid who's always mocking him through the window. But he would also find a way to exact pain on someone who hurt that kid too.

That kid, by the way, is a piece of work! Really. Jeffrey is about 10 years old. He's Bumble's kid. Bumble (not sure how she got the nickname) is a waitress at the diner where I work. It's just the two of them, so Jeffrey is left to his own when mom is at work. Which is a lot.

Let's see, what do you need to know about Bumble? You can tell she's seen some things. You can tell that a lot of those things she would have rather not seen. She's pretty in a road house sort of way. She does what she can. She's a bottle blonde and, based on her roots, a natural brunette. She's got a variety of tattoos, most of which cannot be seen. One that is always visible is across her neck: "Only God Can Judge Me." Which is ironic on a couple of levels. First, the very nature of the tattoo invites judgement. Second, people actually can judge and don't need the judged person's permission to do so. Irregardless, (I know that's not really a word, but I use it because Bumble uses it and especially because that word makes Basil absolutely mental. He just heard me use it and he's going off right now: "You illiterate moron! You should be writing that in crayon! I envy the people that haven't met you!")

Bumble works mainly at the diner, but she also works for a cleaning service on the side. Gotta pay the light bill and get the three food groups on the table: Marlboros, bologna, and bread. So there's not much "parenting" happening with Jeffrey. Jeffrey asks and answers his own questions, which is a frightening prospect for a well-rounded adult, not to mention a 10 year old child. Ever since Basil saw Jeffrey blow up a frog (a trait I assume came from his biological father) he's had his eye on him. It's a short walk from Amphibian to Felidae.

Bumble's parenting style could be best described as "Free Range." Or sub grouped as "Don't Stifle Their Creativity." Resulting in a shared sentiment that Basil and I (along with most of the apartment complex) agree on, which is "We Don't Condone Child Abuse...But..."

Case in point: It's Tuesday morning and it's hotter than donut grease at a fat man convention. Nobody is in the mood for any shit. It's the kind of day that everybody kind of agrees on the universal rule: Nobody moves, nobody talks. Let's all just be still and it'll be over soon. There's only one good thing happening in our little complex right now, and it's that Bill has gone to work and Maggie gets a few hours break. Maggie and Bill have been married for 30 years, only because Maggie couldn't figure out how to kill him or leave him. She would have preferred the first option. Bill is just an asshole. No two ways from it. Born wrong. Taught wrong. And he's relentless with Maggie. He doesn't let up. "Bring me a beer!" "Beer me, bitch!" "Get your fat ass in here Jonsey and clean this mess up!" Jones was her maiden name and he calls her that to remind her of the hell he rescued her from. His perspective.

Bill fights his demons with whiskey and women. And he keeps his tool belt full and his tools sharp. That's a nice way of saying he drinks a lot and he has sex with a lot of women not named Maggie. Bill is no prize, so the "women" he dates could only be described as not-quite-good-enough-for-day-shift strippers. Basil and I like strippers generally, just not the ones that date Bill.

Maggie said that if I had met Bill's parents I'd understand Bill. I guess that's probably true. I'd suppose that if I had met the people who raised Bill's parents that would make sense to me also. All behavior makes sense in context. But just because I understand it doesn't mean I have to tolerate it. But Maggie tolerates it, I guess, because she doesn't see another option. That makes me thing about the people who jumped out of the burning towers on 9/11. Leaving the building in that way was not even a consideration that morning when they showed up for their jobs. And yet, it became a reasonable option to reasonable people. Context is everything.

I've not pried into Maggie's loyalty too much. Mainly because prying invites reciprocity. And I like to be left alone. But I watch Bill like I watch a car wreck. I'm a pretty quick study when it comes to people. I think Malcomb Gladwell called it Rapid Cognition in one of his books. Thin Slicing. Anyway, by my estimation, Bill is afraid of his own shadow. Not only that, but he is profoundly lonely. Now he and I have about the same number of close associates (He has none, I have Basil), but I am just alone. The difference? When you're alone and you don't want to be, that's lonely. When you're alone and it suits you, well, that's pretty sweet. So Bill is angry, sad, lonely, discontent, and drunk. He's basically a Jackson Pollock painting with chicken legs. Basil says he couldn't pour piss out of a boot if the instructions were on the heel. I'd say that's true, and I'd also say Basil is spending too much time on the internet. It's gotta be the internet. But I can't work out how he's navigating that. His paws are bigger than any one key on my laptop. If he ever downloads TikTok we're all fucked.

So when Bill's gone, Maggie gets to sit out in her lawn chair and fan herself in the shade and nurse a lemonade with a little extra zing in it. And this Tuesday it had been particularly rough. Bill must have been constipated because he was grumpier than usual. We all heard it. So after his tirade he left and Maggie finally made it to the chair with her special lemonade and her fan. She plopped down and finally found some peace, and everybody in the complex felt the same collective sigh of relief. Finally, a moment of rest for Maggie (and for us)! It was quiet. Soft as a whisper outside. Almost angelic.

And then, from the open window, we heard the shriek of Jeffrey as he pierced the solace with, "HEY Maggie!!! Show us yer tits!!!" The kid is just feral. No other way to say it.

That sent Maggie inside in a flustered state while the rest of us worked through a cost/benefit analysis of duct taping him to the wall until his mom got home.

The only thing that stopped us was we couldn't find any duct tape. Now, we don't condone child abuse…

Jeffrey doesn't even know what he's yelling. He's heard Bill scream it across the yard at Bumble and few other ladies. And Jeffrey, being without any kind of male role model, is unfortunately left with Bill and Kimball. Kimball needs a walking around helmet, and if you don't know what that is don't bother looking into it. It'll just make your day worse than it already was. Suffice it to say, Kimball isn't in line for any arranged marriages and he's not getting many calls from the sperm bank. The difference between Bill and Kimball is that Kimball is nice. But neither were burdened with excessive intelligence.

I certainly understand Bill wanting to see a pair of quality breasts, given that Maggie's deflated during the Carter administration and look like they're trying to get away from her shoulders. But Jeffrey is headed for a beat down (not from us, because we don't condone…) if he doesn't reign it in.

Basil said, "I've got eight nipples here for you Jeffrey! Come over here and let me show you what cats sometimes do to their young." Basil then mumbled what was arguably his best insult: "Jeffrey, Rick Astley would have given you up for adoption."

Too bad only I heard it.

11.

I read about the Shopping Cart Theory the other day. A guy named Jared on Twitter suggested that what we do with shopping carts could be the best measure of our morality. It goes something like this:

1. Returning a shopping cart is socially accepted as the right thing to do.

2. There is no penalty for NOT returning the cart. No one will fine you or harm you.

3. Nothing is gained by returning your cart.

So, according to the theory, you are a good member of society if you return your cart and a bad member of society if you don't. Like most theories that put people in one of two categories, this one has some gaping flaws in it. The flaw is in the second premise. There is a penalty (for some) in not returning the cart. The possibility, however slight, that one would be seen in an unfavorable light, is more than enough penalty to return the cart. For the theory to be a true test of character, returning the shopping cart would have to be done without the possibility of being observed. Then we would see what someone is made of. Actually, then we would see a parking lot full of carts strewn about. Forgive the pessimism.

I return carts. And I give people the slow eye that don't. But I can't say for certain if I return them because I'm trying to be helpful or if I trying to avoid being judged. It's complicated. That's why Basil is in my life. Basil is a cart returner. Not that he's ever returned a cart, but that's just who he is. He would return the cart because it's efficient. Regardless of who saw him or didn't see him. I know this because he will, regardless of who sees him or not, hike his leg and lick his own ass. He will look you dead in the eye while he does it too. He skips a step that we humans have developed. Since most of us can't lick our own ass, I'll suggest the human equivalent of this is picking our nose. Most people (beyond a certain age) will go through these steps before digging in their own nose:
1. It feels like something is in my nose.
2. Let me look around and see if anybody is watching me.
3. Dig for gold.

Basil skips the second step. Not because he lacks empathy or is incapable of shame, but because he doesn't automatically take the second step. The other day we were watching a cooking show together and Basil just dropped down and started licking his ass, right about the same time that Rachel Ray started making Daddy Wu's Pan Fried Chicken. One of my favorites.

"Basil, seriously???" I said.

"Look Carl. You can look or you can look away. I don't have opposable thumbs so therefore I don't have access to toilet paper. What I do have is a particular set of skills, one of which is a rough tongue and a high tolerance for what lands on it. And an itchy ass. Add to that an extreme level of apathy about your thoughts on the matter. Given those facts, to NOT lick my own ass would be a travesty. So I will not allow you to manufacture shame out of your imposed puritanical values. Now kindly turn your attention back to Rachel so you don't screw up the chicken next time."

Basil says about the time women had to start covering their breasts (and men didn't) things started going downhill from there. No argument from me on that one. On a couple of levels.

12.

Bill came over to borrow a wrench today to fix his washing machine. It's an old model; I'm surprised it's not driven by a steam engine. It breaks often, and he needs the same crescent wrench to fix it each time. And each time he comes over and asks if I have it.

"Yes, Bill. I have it. I still have it. Yes, you can borrow it."

But today Bill does something different. Something unusual. Something so un-Bill like it caused Basil to stop mid-lick on his bath and pay attention.

Bill asked a question. "Carl, we're friends right?"

The social dilemma becomes immediately apparent to me. Quick as lightening I am able to answer the question in five different ways in my head. But I am here. And this is now. And Bill wants to know if we are friends. Stalling, I answer a question with a question.

"Bill, why do you ask?"

Bill said, "Maggie and I had a fight last night and something she said has me wondering. She was complaining about my drinking and she said, 'That's why you don't have any friends.' I told her I had lots of friends. I told her you and I were friends. And then she laughed at me."

Maggie must have slipped a gear last night. She got pretty bold, telling Bill what she thought. Her usual tactic is to stand still and quiet and wait for the storm to pass. I guess last night was different. Bill stood there in front of me, waiting on the answer to his question.

I'd like to lie to Bill. For two reasons. If I told him we were friends he'd be satisfied with that answer (it would mean Maggie is wrong and he is right) and he would leave with the wrench and leave quickly. Bill leaving quickly suits me just fine. But then Basil looked at me with his "You don't have the balls" look, and I decided to take the long way home.

"Bill, the truth is we are not friends. Friends do a couple of things. Friends look after one another, and friends enjoy each other's company. Maggie is my friend, and so is Basil..."

Bill became indignant, "You're friends with a fucking cat??? I don't know what I was thinking coming in here asking a stupid question!"

Basil was flipping him off at this point, but it's hard for most people to tell with his short little fingers. Did you know a cat's front paw has fingers and their back paw has toes? How about that?

I know I can take this conversation one of two ways. I can end it, which I want to do, or I can try to help, which I don't want to do. Not anymore. I'm here, in this place, in part from my helping. If I just call him a dumbass he'll storm out and I won't have to deal with him again. Basil said, "Do it. We've got dinner to make. Plus we're behind on the Bachelor. It's supposed to be the most dramatic episode ever."

I found a middle ground. I looked at Bill, and in a soft tone I said, "Yup, that was a stupid question."

He turned on his heels (with the wrench in his hand) and left in a flash. Basil was doing an end zone dance and said, "My Man! How 'bout some tuna to celebrate!"

Here's the thing. As I'm telling this story you probably had in your mind the way you wanted it to go. Maybe you're under the impression that I'm a good man. But I'm not really. Yes, I take back shopping carts. But I've hurt too many people to be good. The kicker is this: Despite my lack of goodness, sending Bill on his way was the right thing to do for me. Basil knows it. I'm starting to get it. My time is mine and Bill didn't deserve any of it. He has made no deposits into my emotional bank account. In fact, he's overdrawn. And I get to decide what it costs for people to have access to my time. I can also change that cost at my discretion. As a younger man he would have had access to my time and energy. I would have poured it all out for him. Trying to "help." What was I thinking? That the Bills of the world would listen to a few minutes of my compassionate reasoning and just undo 60 years of dysfunction? Eradicate 3 generations of epigenetics? It'd be like trying to blow out a lightbulb.

It took years of therapy and hundreds of hours of painful self-work for me to get to the bottom of some of my issues. It came too late by my estimation. But I can't change that now. But here's what I know. The Bills in my formative years were feared, not respected. I obeyed them for the temporary worth it gave me. I obeyed them in order to avoid being an abject disappointment. So the pattern was set. And when the pastor (who was not a Bill, but resembled a Bill in that he had authority) suggested I "come forward" I did just that. The applause wasn't heady, but it did signal acceptance. Then, when a different pastor (also not a Bill) suggested I "take the next step" and consider the ministry, I did exactly that. More acceptance. I actually didn't have a spiritual experience with God until years later. Never in a church. I met God a few times over the years, mostly in nature or with a small group of people in pain. The truth is I didn't even start thinking about who I was or how I got there until I was well into my 30's. I don't think I gained any insight into my relational patterns until I was well into my 50's. Which put me well ahead of my parents, and their parents. I was simply raised by emotional idiots. They were both raised by emotional idiots. I didn't have much of a chance. I certainly could have dealt with it sooner though. That's my part.

My mother's father was a Bill of a grand scale. He was cartoonishly a Bill. My dad's parents went to great lengths to make sure no one thought they were a Bill. But my Dad's mom was a Bill none the less. Nobody knew.

So as a younger man I used to collect Bills. I sought them out, unaware of what I was doing. What I was doing, as it turns out, was trying to make the ledger sheet balance. My early experiences with Bill types left me feeling unworthy. If I collected a Bill as an adult and they valued me, well, it would prove the childhood Bills were just plain wrong. The problem with my plan was that Bills, by their very nature, collect people just like me. And they use us as playthings. And that didn't do much for my ledger sheet. This is basically the blueprint for trauma. For many people (including myself), trauma is at the heart of our maladaptive behaviors.

When today's Bill closed the door Basil said, "Fuck 'em. Soooo. Tuna?"

"Yeah, Basil. Tuna it is." I wondered how my life would have been different if I had learned how to be kind to myself at a younger age. Who knows? The important thing, I guess, is that I know now.

13.

My Personal History of Bills (might as well get into it):

Bill #1 was a drunk and abusive to most people. Because he abused me less frequently, people said he favored me. He was raised by people who didn't know much about relationships. In fact, I suspect they kept some pretty dark secrets. My great aunt had a "car accident" when she was still a fairly young woman. I suspect she learned something about her family that made the guardrail seem like the better option. She was always kind to me, and I always felt safer when she was around. She acted like she was protecting me from something. I'm glad I'll never know what that was.

Bill #1 didn't try to hide his narcissism. He also had never heard that word before. I'd say he cared about me as much as he was able, but he really lacked any ability to connect with people on a personal level. He collected people for tasks and didn't hide that from anybody. That might be why his wife, in one last act of defiance, chose to be buried far away from him. She was given about 20 years after his death to forgive him, but I don't think 100 years would have been enough.

Bill #2 was a female. She took great pains to make sure no one ever thought she had ever done anything wrong ever. In fact, if it became known that you had done something wrong, she would distance herself (without saying so) so as not to be guilty by implication. To most people she was kind and gentle and good. To some, like her husband, she cracked the whip. I never knew what she was thinking or feeling. She never let anyone know. You would ask her a question, and you could see her running through all of the possible answers in her head and, like a multiple choice test, choosing the option that put her in the best light.

Being a generation removed, I never felt her scorn, but I watched her dish it out to her husband. And I watched her sons cower in fear of her displeasure.

Bill #3 was a band director. Brash, loud, demanding. He made no bones about your worth as a human. If you played the right note at the right time with the right volume, you are worthy. If you didn't, you weren't. Like it is with all Bills, pleasing him became important to me. When he told me I was playing well it meant the world to me. Winning a national championship was second to his reaction to the trophy.

By the time I had gone through three Bills I had become familiar with a pattern. Find someone who was not exactly emotionally available and win their favor. If I did that, then it could erase the previous Bill's wounds. It made me feel like a person.

Bills #4 and #5 were so identical that they don't deserve differentiation. Spoiled, pretending to be humble servants, micro managers, compliance was their oxygen. They were my introduction to covert narcissists. Pastors and therapists make up this lot. These are people that are pretending to be good. But they're not. They pose as Godly, benevolent beings. They are not. They need a constant supply of blind adoration and if someone dare question their intelligence or methods, they are discarded. They have no peers and no friends. It looks like they have both. But the peers and friends are held together by fear or money. Often both. Their displeasure is so uncomfortable. Rational people will do irrational things just to avoid their scorn.

Even right now as I write this, Basil and I are watching impeachment proceedings on the president. He's never been accused of being covert about his narcissism, but it is interesting watching the Republicans right now. There's no way they believe what they're saying at the podium.

I asked Basil, "I wonder how many people who are fervent Trump supporters have been hurt by a narcissist in their past?"

"Yeah," Basil said. "That'd be all of them I think."

Ross Rosenberg pretty much nailed it concerning covert narcissists:

"Compared to overt narcissists, covert narcissists are more reserved and composed. By not advertising their deeper narcissistic values and motives, they are able to achieve their goals, while protecting their innermost insecurities and vulnerabilities. Unlike overt narcissists, they expend a great deal of psychological energy containing or hiding their callous, indifferent, and manipulative inner selves. Even though covert narcissists have repressed the full scope and magnitude of their personality disorder, on a semi-conscious level, they are aware that their fantasies are embarrassing and unacceptable.

"Because covert narcissists are able to create and maintain a facade of altruism and unconditional positive regard, they are able to function in positions that are traditionally not attractive to narcissists, e.g., clergy, teachers, politicians, psychotherapists and others. Even though they are able to replicate the known characteristics of these positions, they are often deeply insecure and secretive about their lack of knowledge or inability to perform the most essential tasks. For example, a covert narcissist who is a psychotherapist will have mastered the stereotypical career-specific, idiosyncratic behavior patterns such as reflective listening, supporting and accepting feedback, and gestures that mimic unconditional acceptance. However, this covert narcissist psychotherapist will be deficient in the most critical area of the job. Although they attempt to demonstrate honesty, sympathy and empathy with their clients, they ultimately fall short.

They are simply unable to master the key elements of the position, as they are inherently judgmental, controlling and emotionally aloof. These therapists often become agitated at their clients when challenged or questioned. Clients who do not let them control the process will often trigger a narcissistic injury.

"These secretive and slippery narcissists react to their unmasking with the full force of their arsenal of weapons that you would never guess existed. When they perceive a threat to their carefully and meticulously crafted public persona, all bets are off! Since their personal and professional reputation is built on a foundation of lies and misrepresentations, they will protect it by any means necessary. Their reflex to attack the perceived threat is fueled by an adrenaline-infused survival instinct that is no different than if they were cornered by a pack of hungry wolves. They will try to crush the threat, while positioning themselves as the victim of a premeditated vindictive and grievous harm."

Where was Ross when I needed him most?

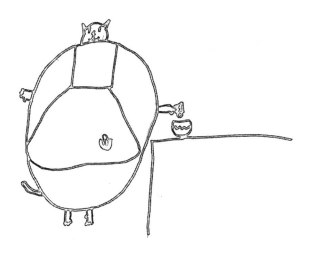

14.

Basil and I are pretty apolitical. In 2020 this effectively alienates us from everyone. Which suits us just fine. Basil and I also agree on this: Trump is at least a Bill. He probably has some other things going on, most of which I blame on his father. One good thing about his presidency (maybe the only good thing) is that he has emboldened the idiots. They have slithered out from the rocks and shown themselves. Important People have told them they are right. I'm thankful that we know them now.

Basil said, "Do you remember the good old days? When idiots at least knew enough to keep their damn mouths shut?"

Basil and I were speechless, watching the terrorists storm Capitol Hill. Waving the confederate flag. Five deaths. This asshole is responsible for this act of sedition.

At least now we know who is who. Or at least it's clearer. Thank God Basil doesn't have opposable thumbs. He has asked me countless times to be his scribe for a Twitter account. I can't imagine that cat if he actually had followers. He'd be intolerable.

Regardless of your political affiliation, let's just agree on two things: First, Trump is grossly incompetent. He never wanted to be president and never developed the skill set for it. In fact, if you want to blame somebody for his presidency, blame Obama. Now, Basil and I are huge Obama fans. Every time I catch Basil leaving the shit box he kind of saunters out and says, "That's what I do!" Sounds just like Obama when he hit that 3 pointer with Steph Curry. But Obama triple dog dared Trump. The one thing that Bills hate, loathe actually, is to be mocked. Belittled. If it's in public, that's the pinnacle of offense. And Obama did exactly that. Trump was a guest at the White House Correspondents dinner and Obama had had enough. He uncorked on him. Go watch the video, I'll wait 'til you get back. You can see it in Trump's face. That moment steeled his resolve.

That he got elected is another issue, mostly having to do with the convergence of our growing skill of keeping stupid people alive and the blossoming of the internet. Regardless of your views, there's thousands of people on the internet that will agree with you. Do you think Justin Bieber is actually a Lizard Person? Might as well look that up too. It's a thing. That has followers. In the thousands. The vaccine has a microchip? Seriously. I'm starting to get an idiot headache. I need a break.

When I'm feeling a little stressed and I need a pick me up, now that cocaine is off the menu, I'll turn on Harry Styles' version of Sledgehammer he did on the Howard Stern Show. Since we're looking stuff up tonight, give it a go. When I put that on, doesn't matter what time of day or night. Doesn't matter if Basil is awake or asleep or in mid shit. Basil will drop what he is doing and begin this trance like dance to that song. He says it's an eargasm. Musical perfection. He's not wrong. But that dance! I never did acid and I never saw the Grateful Dead, but I imagine it must have been something like what I'm watching Basil doing. I wish I had something like that. Something that could short circuit reality and transport me to a place like that. I've tried various substances, but that only works short term. I've tried religious euphoria, but it never took.

I remember being in a church service where the euphoria was being passed out like Chiclets. I tried it, it wasn't for me, so I ended up just watching people. This one lady really got there. Spinning, spinning, crying, and shaking. She ended up on the floor shaking her hands violently. One by one, her rings started to fling off her hands like shrapnel. She had on a lot of rings. At that moment you could tell who in that room was experiencing true religious ecstasy and who was just rubber necking. The rubber-neckers, of whom I was a member, started dodging flying rings as they pinged off the windows and ceiling. And we were amused. Trying to hide our smiles and giggles from the faithfully ecstatic was a chore. Somebody leaned over to me and said, "I'm headed for the door. Cover me!" That was a good time for sure. The ring flinger reminds me of Basil listening to that song. OK, I've gone down a rabbit hole. Back to Cheeto.

The second thing that seems true about Trump: Being in any kind of relationship with him must be a complete nightmare. Spouse, child, cabinet member. Can you imagine being his Vice President? I can. I have been, a few times. Here's their dirty little secret, and every Bill will deny this to their last dying breath, but it's the truth: Bills will communicate in an intentionally vague and confusing way because watching their supply try to "break the code" is their favorite past time. This is why most Bills are micromanagers; they like to be catered to.

Basil pointed out this is why Trump doesn't have a dog: "Dogs are simple creatures, not given to complexities. Sure, they're loyal if you show even the slightest hint of love, but some people don't have any love to give. With no love to offer, Dogs become disinterested. Which looks like apathy. Which Trump would hate. And there's no way Trump would have a cat. Cats are, by nature, discerning creatures. We are literate and we think for ourselves. I read a tweet by @crandallgold the other day, 'If you think that Mexico is only sending drug dealers and rapists, but also worry that Mexicans are going to take your job, what the fuck do you do for a living?' You see, Carl, I get that. A Labrador wouldn't. Beautiful breed, though."

15.

I dislike panhandlers. Every time Basil sees one on TV he says, "Those greasy fuckers make bank." He doesn't mean greasy as in unkempt. He means greasy as in they probably have a nice car parked around the corner.

I was leaving work yesterday and a panhandler was waiting for me. I don't know if I just seem approachable, but I have worked hard for the better part of four decades to reverse that. I certainly don't give off the vibe that I have a lot of walking around money. For whatever reason, they guy asks for a dollar. It went like this:

"Dude, got a spare buck?"

"Not really," I said. "Don't really have a spare anything."

He persisted, "Seriously, not even a dollar? You got no heart!"

Well now that pissed me off. I'm not sure how me not giving him a dollar for nothing in return equates to an evaluation of my benevolence. Whatever, we're locked in now.

"Actually I have both a dollar and a heart, but I'm used to getting something for my money. I could get a hot cup of coffee for this dollar, what would you give me?"

He hung his head a little, "I ain't got nothin'. That's why I'm out here." He started to walk away, but now I am in a mood.

"Hey wait, I've got an idea. Sometimes I pay for entertainment. You got any jokes?"

"Yes!" he said. "Why did the chicken cross the road?"

I shook my head, "Nah, that's not funny. Got any other ways to be entertaining?"

He dropped his head again, knowing I was taking the piss. I had an idea.

"Hey, do you know how to dance?"

"Yes," he said. "I sure do!"

"Well, let see what you got?"

He looked confused, "I don't have any music..."

I shot back, "Looks like you'll have to sing as well."

Sing and dance he did. Both poorly, but I gave him a dollar anyway.

I asked him, "So tell me how you feel about yourself."

"Like shit," he said.

I replied, "Me too."

The exchange reminded me of a time when I was a boy. I was having lunch at the diner with Bill #1 when an African American man came through the door. In that time, in that part of the country, that was fairly uncommon. He and Bill #1 locked eyes and Bill #1 said, "You can come in, but you have to dance first." And so he did. Bill #1 had a reputation of hurting people when he didn't get what he wanted. That was my first experience with racism. Sadly, it was not my last.

Bill #1 taught me a lot about how not to treat people.

But maybe you see the difference? Bill #1 did this in front of people. I was taught that Bill #2 was the better model, and she modeled hiding the flaw. Looking back, if I had followed in Bill #1's footsteps I would have been dead or fixed a very long time ago.

Only the stark light of day has ever corrected my defects. That and a willingness to change. And I only change when I believe that the change will improve the quality of my life. If you think that's selfish you've not explored your own motives for change very well.

16.

One of the reasons we are slow to change is because we tend to be the most transparent around the people who are least objective about us.

17.

Bumble stopped by the other day for a chat. Which always means two things. First, she is bringing something over for Basil. And second, she needs to talk. Today, she brought Basil a catnip toy. He looked at that toy they way I looked at the Farah Fawcett poster in 1976. Welp, there goes Basil. I'll not see him the rest of the afternoon.

I don't entertain guests, and I don't look forward to visitors. But Bumble is different. She's more like family in that I don't clean up for her and she can use whatever glass is clean in the kitchen if she gets thirsty. I don't offer to get her a drink.

"What's up, Bumble? Take a load off," I said, gesturing toward the couch.

"Not much Carl. Hey, can I ask you a question?" she wondered aloud.

I don't understand people asking if they can ask a question. I guess it's a form of manners? Usually it signifies a heavy subject, and today was no exception.

"Give it to me straight, Carl. What's wrong with me?" she pleaded.

Bumble and I have this conversation from time to time. It's almost scripted. It always comes on the heels of her getting disappointed by some asshole. Actually, I really can't think of what might be wrong with Bumble. She's smart, attractive, has a great sense of humor, and she's organically kind. Meaning she's kind even when she's not being observed. I saw her walking along the sidewalk one day and she jumped straight up in the air. She turned around and bent down and picked up some kind of worm shaped creature and relocated it to a place with less foot traffic. She didn't know I was watching. But that's when I started inviting her over.

"Who did it and what did he do?" I sighed as I fell back into my chair.

"Well," she sighed, "This one's name is Clint and he was doing fine. No face tattoos, not currently on probation, has a job, bathes regularly. A real dream boat."

"Go on," I probed.

She blurted it out, "He asked if I'd be down for a threesome with his ex!"

Basil flew around the corner at that point looking like he just found a mouse in a coma. "Well, here I am!! What were your other two wishes??" Catnip makes him crazy!

I can't talk to Basil when someone is there, mainly because I don't want to go to the psych ward. These are moments Basil loves, because he can get away with just about anything. It allows him to play his favorite game, which is try to get me to react visibly to something he says in front of company, which would no doubt confuse the other person. Like if I laughed out loud but nothing was said. I hate this game, but there's really no stopping it.

Basil continued, "I'm down for a threesome! I'm pretty sick of the onesomes!" Now that about got me. Basil staggering around drunk on catnip is a sight of its own. But him slurring words is priceless. Gotta keep it together, because tonight's topic is not exactly light.

Back to Bumble, "So what'd you tell him?"

Bumble shot back, "I told him to get fucked, which he said that's exactly what he was trying to do!"

I told Bumble I was sorry, that nothing is wrong with her, that there are plenty of fish in the sea, and that any guy would be lucky to be with her.

"Oh yeah?" she countered. "Then tell me why, after all this time, you've never hit on me. Not once!"

Basil chimed in, "Yeah Romeo, tell her! I can't wait to hear this one! I've been trying to hook you two up from the start!"

"Well, Bumble," I began. "That's kind of a long story."

She said, "I've got nothing but time!"

18.

One of the good things and one of the shitty things is that I have a large capacity to feel things. I remember finding a baby bird once, almost dead. I tried chest compressions and fresh water and shade, but the baby bird died, despite my efforts. That shook me for a whole day. So I've got a 55 gallon feel bucket.

The first essay I remember writing in grade school was a first person story told from the perspective of the unborn child. I was empathizing with a fetus. It was cinematic!

My depression, when it shows up, resembles Jung's Collective Unconscious. I can feel all of the pain I've seen in my life. Losing people and pets as a child. The pain others have felt when they have been abused or rejected. The invisible people. It feels like my Amygdala is in an Instant Pot.

But I can also feel joy and happiness on the same level. That feels like magic.

I wouldn't trade my deep feelings for anything. I've felt things through nature and music and human connection that many people have only read about. But the down side is that it can also cause deep hurt. And I have loved a woman in a way that the universe designed. And it was unrequited. She tried to love me, but she loved another more. Not worth the details, but the part of my bucket that contained romantic love was cut off from the blood supply. I experienced romantic cyanosis.

The truth is that Bumble is exactly the kind of woman I would fall for if I were able. Spunky, sexy, caring. But I have no room. That part of me is dead. And I'm not particularly upset about it. During the years when I was with her (her name is Rose) I probably lived two years for every chronological year. I don't wish for more. Exhibit A: I just found out that Olivia Wilde is available and I felt nothing. Case closed.

Love is an absolute consequence of beauty, and she was truly beautiful. You know you're in love when your wants and needs become invisible compared to hers. She was all I thought about. How to anticipate her wants and needs. Her pleasure brought me more pleasure than my own. A clinical person would say I was "obsessed" and that it wasn't "healthy." Well, they can "kiss my ass." It was the God particle of my existence. It's over. And it was such an amazing experience that I'm not even sad it's over. The only lasting sting is that she had a lesser experience than I did. I sure wish that wasn't so.

Bumble sat in silence and she heard my long answer. After I finished, she waited a minute more and then interrupted the quiet with this: "So you DO think I'm attractive!!"

She seemed pleased, and frankly I'm used to not being really heard, so I wasn't too disappointed. Being vulnerable has never returned much for me anyway.

Basil came in again and I could tell the catnip was wearing off a little, and he directed his next observation toward Bumble:

"Just because I'm smiling doesn't mean I'm glad you're here."

I'm glad she couldn't hear that. I'm glad nobody can hear Basil except me.

I know that means it's time to not have company any longer. Basil has a few other tricks up his paw in case I didn't get the hint. Having company for both of us is like a fish out of water. So I stand up and walk toward the door. Bumble gets the hint and follows me.

"Thanks Carl, you're the best," she said as she leaned in for a hug. "Bye, Basil!"

Basil thanked her for the catnip and started to get ready for his nightly routine. I closed the door and breathed in deeply. Finally, safe again. I did look through the blinds and watched her walk away. Basil's right, she's a good looking woman.

Basil said, "Did you see that dump truck??"

"No, Basil, I did not see a dump truck (Yes I did)."

Basil continued, "Carl, my man, you have to get back out there! You're not too far gone to rally!"

I don't say anything to Basil. He responds predictably to extinction. And I'm not in a place to have the conversation. I'm not in a place to ever have it, really. Talking about it now I'm welling up. I can smell her and taste her. I can remember exactly how her back felt when I put my hand on it. How she used to breathe deeply when she was completely contented. How she would turn down the right corner of her mouth when she wasn't getting what she wanted when she wanted it.

You can call it whatever you want. Love. Dependence. It makes no difference to me. I glad it happened. I wish it was still happening. I'm uninterested in it happening with anyone else. Because that is an impossibility.

Love is blind, isn't it? I didn't know what I know now for years. I just thought if I tried a little harder everything would be OK. I couldn't have been more wrong than that.

The truth is I've had my last first kiss.

19.

When I woke up today there sat Basil staring at me. He had a look on his face that said, "I should knock the shit out of this motherfucker right now!" When I looked at the clock I understood. Breakfast was an hour late. Basil is actually quite pleasant unless he's uncomfortable. That includes angry, tired, warm, cold, hungry, and constipated. So Basil doesn't know how to self soothe very well.

I guess neither did Henry David Thoreau: "Know your own bone; gnaw at it, bury it, unearth it, and gnaw still."

That doesn't sound like a very peaceful existence to me at all. I'm all for self-examination, but come on. All that gnawing and burying and unearthing and re-gnawing. That sounds exhausting.

These days I find moving with the current pretty soothing. I've spent the better part of my adult life trying to alter the course of a river. But, as it turns out, water seeks its own level with or without me. Talk about an exercise in futility.

Basil has finished breakfast and he's been to the shit box, so he's lost that homicidal look in his eye. At least for now. Give him a couple of hours. For me it's off to work. Make the dirty dishes clean. I really do like this job. There are zero surprises waiting for me. The dishes will, in fact, be dirty. And I will, by machine or by hand, make them clean using a simple set of repetitive skills. I don't have to learn anything. I am free from the request of vulnerability. I am free to daydream. To hypnotize myself for 8 hours. Most days I will forget to take a lunch. Some days I'll forget to go to the bathroom. I should have been a factory worker from the start. But being a dreamer got in the way of that. Oh well. Mutatis mutandis.

When I was younger I dreamed of changing the world. That idea didn't originate with me. I was told that by a few people. I was once called a "garbanzo de a Libra." One of a kind. I hope those people didn't spend a lot of money on the stock market, because they weren't particularly astute at predictions. The cliff notes of it all is that I didn't change the world. But I can change a shit box. Basil and I call it a shit box because that's what it is. Technically, a shit'n'piss box, but that's too long. Point is, it's not litter. Basil gets worked up sometimes about the names of things.

Basil has always had a bit of an anxiety disorder. It got bad last year and he developed psychogenic alopecia. Basically, he got so nervous his hair started to fall out. He had a hard time with that. I don't know if you have had any experience with anxiety, but the bitch about anxiety is, if you have it, you're anxious about it. You have anxiety about having anxiety. So Basil was hard to live with during that time. One day in particular comes to mind.

I remember bringing up the idea gently: "Hey Basil, have you given any thought to maybe talking to someone about it? You know, a professional?"

He was already wound up tighter than a clam's ass at high tide. This set him over the edge.

"A THERAPIST???? You want me to go talk to a therapist?? Have you noticed I'm a fucking cat?!? Your Slinky's kinked! Did you come up with that idea all your own?? Your mom must be proud! Your intellect is rivaled only by garden tools! I'm not going to a fucking therapist for two fucking reasons,"-hair is flying everywhere now, he's getting balder by the second-"First, there are no cat therapists! Second, I'm not going to a fucking therapist!!!"

I guess my timing or my delivery must have been off. Probably both.

I need to stop trying to give solutions to someone who doesn't think they have a problem. That's never worked for me. I'm trying to help. I'm pretty sure I can help.

But he didn't ask me what I thought. Lesson learned, again. I doubt the lesson will stick, though.

I remember trying to get my mom help several times over the years. I called the doctor who was prescribing her happy pills once. I kindly informed him that my mom was abusing the medication and would he be so kind as to stop prescribing the poison. He agreed and thanked me for calling. The next week a fresh bottle of pills showed up in her room. The time for talking was gone. I took a baseball bat up to the doctor's office and tapped it (lightly) on the counter while people scrambled behind the glass. I said I'd like to emphasize to the doctor that he is prescribing lethal medication to my mother. I said I brought the baseball bat because apparently they didn't hear me last time.

Did you know it's generally a bad idea to make a point with a bat? If not, you heard it here first.

I never was able to help my mom. Looking back on it, I was really trying to help myself. I wanted a different kind of mom. She and I are a lot alike. Big appetites. Leap then look. Artistic. Driven by feeling. But I always wondered what it would be like to have a mom who wasn't distracted. In truth, Little Debbie was her favorite child. Who can measure up to that?

Back to Basil...

There's a vet that frequents the diner and I asked him what to do. The next time he came in he gave me a couple of buspirone pills for Basil to try. Turns out that did the trick. He just needed something to break the cycle for a bit. But even then he was prone to ruminate. I've tried to offer other ways to help him relax. I've suggested yoga, meditation, mindfulness, CBT, Tai Chi. He responds to every suggestion the same: "How about you get me a pack of smokes and some bacon and we'll call it good." Smart ass.

The vet suggested a follow up visit and I agreed. I should have consulted Basil about this, but this is new territory for me. Basil wasn't very pleased when I told him he had a visit to the vet that day.
"Great," he said. "What do they want now? They took my balls last time I was there. Do you think they want an eye, or maybe a leg?"

I take his point, but I reminded him that we are doing to a new, friendlier vet, not the ball collector.

So we arrive at the vet and get him registered. They give me some paperwork to fill out and at the top of the sheet is his name. Except it is spelled, "Bazil." I'm not sure what person could misspell "Basil" but apparently they work at the vet.

Basil wasn't having it. "Carl, they spelled my name wrong."

I whispered, "I know Basil. No big deal. I'll take care of it another time."

Basil insisted if he was going to be humiliated the very least they could do was spell his name right. So I approached the girl behind the counter.

"Can you change his name on this form?" I asked. "He doesn't spell it that way."

I guess that was an odd thing to say, as most pet owners name and spell their pet's name any way they like. That could explain the cat named, "Clitsy." I wish I was making that up.

She grinned at me and said, "So how does he spell it?"

"B.A.S.I.L.," I said, slowly.

"Does he have a middle name?" She inquired.

Basil looked me dead in the eye and said, "Tell her my middle name us püppie, and make sure she adds the umlot."

I said, "His middle name is Edward, after Edward Cullen." (Basil despises Twilight).

"And a last name?" She asked.

Basil smiled, "It's Katniss-Neverclean. Don't forget the hyphen."

"Vincent," I said. "His last name is Vincent."

I really can't take him anywhere. He's incessant. And to think, if I hadn't left my helping profession and come out here to Elko I could have missed all of this! A good choice. Rare, but good.

Occasionally I miss being a counselor. People let me in pretty quick, and they gave me a front row seat to the carnage and then the repair. I loved watching a comeback. I don't think I ever hurt a client. If I did, I don't know about it. But I sure hurt people while I was a counselor. That's why the governing body decided I needed a little rest from my profession. One of the things I absolutely love about my life now is that there is no governing body for dishwashers.

I'm glad Basil responded well to the pills. I guess we all get in a cycle sometimes. We just need something to shake us loose. That's always been the hard part for me. When I'm in a dark place all I want is the same things. A dark room, to remain undisturbed, and a sandwich (plain). My dark seasons have been longer than they needed to. If I could just get outside. Talk to somebody. Exercise. That's really the best medicine. Or a pack of smokes and some bacon. Whatever works.

It wasn't long before Basil was back is usual form. I was reading the paper one morning when something caught my eye (after I read about Cheeto's second impeachment).

"Hey Basil," I said. "Here's an interesting article! The headline reads, 'Today is National Dress Up Your Pet Day'!"

I waited, wondering.

"I wish a motherfucker would!!" Basil hissed. "Hey Carl, you know what's funny about that? That holiday comes the day before 'National Piss in Your Human's Ear While They're Sleeping Day'!"

Glad he's back.

Side note, I know most people refer to themselves as pet "owners." I made the same mistake when Basil and I first met. I asked him early on if I was being a good owner.

He said, "Owner?? Bitch, Abraham Lincoln would like a word. Besides, who cleans whose shit around here? Have you ever thought it might be the other way around? Who works? Who puts food in my bowl? Who charges the laptop at night so I can get on the internet when you're gone?"

I interrupted his speech, "So you ARE getting on the internet!! I knew it! But how? You can't type with your paws!"

Basil slow eyed me, "Siri, bitch!"

20.

Basil and I were reading about the Barkley. Have you heard about this race? The Barkley marathon originated in the mind of Lazarus Lake Cantrell when, hearing that assassin James Earl Ray only covered 8 miles in 55 hours after his escape from Brushy Mountain State Penitentiary, stated he bet he could do 100 miles. The marathon is named for Cantrell's friend, Barry Barkley.

It's an insane race by any standards. 100 miles. In the woods. Over 60,000 feet of vertical climb. Since its inception in 1986, 55% of the annual races have had no one complete the course. One guy, Jared Campbell, completed the race three times. In 2014 and 2016, he was the only person to do so. The year in between? Nobody finished.

Did I mention that you have to find between 9 and 14 books in designated locations and tear out the page that corresponds to your race number? Did I mention that the trail is unmarked?? If you're new to the race you simply must follow someone. There's no way around it. And that's just what Jared did. He completed his second race without following someone and when he started his third he noticed something different: there was a group of about 4 or 5 first timers following him around the course. Seems like a pretty good description of life if you ask me.

Here's what Jared had to say about life lessons: "There are lessons in life that can only be learned through fairly massive deviations from our normal, comfortable routines. They can sharpen our optimism and generate a deeper appreciation for the simple things in life."

This is my massive deviation. My life is radically different than in years past. I have no audience. I have no group of people that I am trying to help. I am no longer a helper of any kind. I am alone. I am invisible, mostly. Nondescript. A face in the crowd. You know those "In Memoriam" slide shows they play at the end of every year? They put up pictures of people that changed the world. I always feel bad during those segments. Inevitably, some people get more applause than others. Luke Perry died in 2019. So did Bushwick Bill.

You probably don't know Bushwick. Pancreatic cancer finally got him, but he had a close call in 1991 when, under the influence of PCP, Everclear, and an argument with his girlfriend, he "accidentally" shot himself in the eye. Born in Jamaica with Dwarfism, I'd venture that Bushwick never had an easy way of it.

So Basil and I are watching the ball drop a while back. Everybody shouts for Luke Perry, who, as far as I know, was a helluva guy. Gone too soon. But Bushwick comes up and there's a slight murmuring. At least he made the lineup. How many people didn't make the cut? Moreover, how many people died without anybody noticing at all? Applause is nothing more than a valuation of worth by a group of assembled people.

Bushwick said something cool about his upcoming death, and I found it soothing. During that 1991 "PCP shot to the eye" thing his heart stopped briefly. He said he wasn't afraid to die now that he knows what's on the other side. He didn't elaborate, but it sounds like it's an upgrade.

Thinking about Bushwick makes me consider the differences between acceptance and approval. To gain approval, one must behave in a way that pleases the palate of another. But acceptance has nothing to do with behavior or performance.

So my massive deviation is this: Finally, self-acceptance. Not tied to the approval of others. Content to validate myself and know that everything is going to be OK.

All my life I've sought the approval of others. In fact, self-acceptance was the direct result of the approval of others.

What if approval was the result of self-acceptance? I can hardly imagine it!

And I have a helluva imagination.

21.

The professor came in the diner today. I don't know if
he is actually a professor or if he's ever taught a class in
his life. But he wears a lot of corduroy, and it's Nevada,
so one would assume. His name is Norman and that's
really all we know about him. He's a big guy but you
can tell he's gentle. His hands would tell you he's not
afraid of manual labor but that's not how he makes a
wage.

According to Bumble he's been coming to the diner for
years, a couple times a month. He sits in the same
booth. Orders the same meal. Leaves the same tip.
Hardly ever says a word. But he listens to everything.
And every once in a while he'll just drop a nugget of

wisdom right in your lap. When he does say something, usually to Bumble, she comes back in the kitchen and writes it down so she can remember it word for word. We have a clipboard in back on the wall where we keep all of his quotes.

I'd imagine Norman would be both surprised and embarrassed if he knew we were keeping a clipboard on him. But that's just a guess based on observation. I've never actually talked to the man.

Bumble was complaining about Nevada not having the lottery, and going on about how many of her problems would be solved if she could win a Powerball. Since she's been banned for life from the Casinos (a story she has not fully revealed to us, but swears it was a huge misunderstanding), the lottery would be the next big solution.

She was by the pie counter thinking out loud, "I could get a new car, pay off the hospital bills, get a new house, maybe a few upgrades," - she gestured toward her body - "and then I could get a decent man and maybe not have to work 60 hours a week! Maybe put my life back together!"

Norman was slowly eating his pie when Bumble came by to refill his coffee. That's when he cracked this open: "Things falling apart is a kind of testing and also a kind of healing. We think that the point is to pass the test or to overcome the problem, but the truth is that things don't really get solved. They come together and they fall apart. Then they come together again and fall apart again. It's just like that."

Bumble ran to the back and wrote it down, word for word. When she went back to give him his check he wanted to clarify something.

Nathan said, "Those aren't my words. They belong to Pema Chodron, a favorite author of mine."

He didn't expect a response, paid his bill and left.

I stared at the clipboard for the rest of the shift. One phrase seemed to be in bold font for me: "They come together and they fall apart." And I could see my life superimposed over that quote. Times of coming together and times of falling apart. Time of great grief and striving trying to unfuck the chicken (in case you don't know, you can't unfuck the chicken). Followed by times of incredible ease and flow.

I wondered if I might be having a heart attack, only because my life was flashing before my eyes. So many times of falling apart. More falling apart than coming together. There was so much pain in the deconstruction. The healing was always longer and more painful than the injury. And then times of coming together. I can count about five times in my life when I felt in complete concert with the universe.

One in particular (I'll keep the other four to myself): I had come to the end of my drinking. I had been drinking every two hours around the clock for months. I wasn't drinking to feel good any more. I was drinking to feel like shit, as opposed to feeling like complete shit. Who knew there were degrees of shit? Every morning I played the game called "I Wonder Where I Pissed Last

Night." It's not a popular board game for a reason. I was watching another episode of Friends, one I had seen a thousand times. It was just as unfunny as it was the first time I saw it. I wanted to punch Ross in his smug face. And who does Chandler think he is? Really? Don't get me started on Joey and Phoebe.

I hated everything about me, including my existence. I wanted to no longer exist. When a person hates themselves, they hate everything around them. "Friends" is actually a good show. Obviously. I mean, who wants to punch Joey except a person who can't stand to be near himself?

I'd rather not even write what I did next, I'm still ashamed of it. But I found the bottom. And it's not a trampoline. It's made of hard, cold granite.

And then it happened. God held me. It was not a religious experience like you hear about or read about. I didn't have a vision and I didn't hear anything worthy of a stone tablet. Nothing I could start a religion on. It was an embrace. She lifted me off the granite into her warm arms and sang me a lullaby and rocked me back and forth. My soul warmed and I felt loved and light as a feather. I was enveloped, like in a sleeping bag. Actually, not a sleeping bag. A womb. And I knew, in that moment, that everything was going to be OK.

I didn't drink again for a long time. The embrace left as quickly as it arrived, and I never felt it again. But I didn't need to. The next seven days of detox were hell, but I held onto the embrace, and it made everything tolerable.

The memory of that day, if I choose to access it, is as strong as the day it happened. Every time I hear the song I'm jolted back to that day when I ran into the end of myself. "You are my sunshine, my only sunshine..." That's the song God sang to me.

The same song my aunt sang to me when I was an infant. I remember her rocking me in a chair and singing me that song, long before a memory should have been formed. God was there, then, and here, now. The beginning and the end.

When I got back home, after I fed Basil, I looked up the quote. The professor only gave us part of it. Pema Chodron continued, "The healing comes from letting there be room for all of this to happen: room for grief, for relief, for misery, for joy."

And so as a young man I can see how almost everything I did was in anticipation of avoiding painful emotions. Now, as a man of a certain age, I can hold both the misery and the joy, sometimes at the same time. I only wish it hadn't cost so much to learn this.

22.

It's Sunday and Basil and I are participating in our weekly religious ceremony. I'm eating a bowl of cereal and Basil is lapping at a bowl of milk and we are watching funny animal videos on the educational channel. The bend of the Earth must be lined up, because the rabbit ears are producing an unusually clear picture today. Same Sunday as the Sunday before and the Sunday before that. Basil and I love the comfort of routine.

There's a video of a guy grabbing a kitten's belly and the kitten is laying on his back and when the guy grabs him the kitten throws his legs wide and spreads his paws. Maybe you've seen it? Anyway, just a normal

Sunday until Basil breaks the sound barrier with a squeal.

"What in the fuck is that???" Basil shrieked. "Seriously, Carl, what in the finger fuck am I looking at??? Watch it!! Carl, look!! I'm serious!! What kind of sorcery am I watching???"

Basil is looking at the video, which is repeating several times because, I don't know, they didn't have enough kitten videos this week? Or they thought it would be funnier the more times we watch it? But now Basil is on his back, staring at his front paws and then looking at the screen and then back to his paws.

"Carl, quick, how many toes do you see on the screen?? Basil squealed. "COUNT THEM!!!"

I thought Basil might have contracted Toxoplasma Gondii for a minute. The video ended but I quickly found it online and watched it a few times.

I started counting, "One, two, three, four, five. I see five."

Basil was frothing at the mouth now, and I was wondering if he might have turned. I wondered if zombie cats were fast or slow.

"COUNT THEM AGAIN!!!" he screamed.

I came up with the same number, and said so to Basil. At which point he fainted dead away. I wasn't too worried about it, as Basil was given to bouts of fainting, both real and concocted for his benefit. So I waited until he stirred, but he was clearly in distress. I asked him what could possibly be the matter.

He was stammering now, much quieter, "I…..am……" - labored breathing intensifies signaling a possible Oscar performance - "deformed." And he fell over again, clearly in distress. OK, maybe this wasn't an act.

"Basil," I said. "Tell me what's wrong!"

Basil rolled over and made eye contact with me for a brief second and then looked away. He held out his right front paw as an exhibit, and said, "I have six toes! Which means either that kitten is deformed or I am, and they wouldn't put a deformed kitten on TV, so it must be me!"

I knelt down next to him and counted his toes and Basil was right. Six toes (fingers? dewclaw?) on the right front. Five toes on the left front. Four toes each on the back. He's got one extra digit.

"Look it up! Quick! I want to know how long I have… to live" he whimpered.

I told Basil I was sure that it wasn't terminal, but we would look it up together. Turns out it has a name: Polydactyly...

Basil screams, "I knew it!!!"

I continued, "And it's acquired in an autosomal dominant manner…"

Basil screaming still, "I've never even met a cat named Autosomal in my life!!"

I was reading right off the wiki page, which in hindsight was not a great idea. I got to the part where is says, "Some cases of polydactyly are caused by mutations in the ZRS, a genetic enhancer that regulates expression of the Sonic Hedgehog (Shh) gene in the limb."

Game over.

Basil starts screaming, "I'm a mutant hedgehog!!! I'm a MUTANT Hedgehog??? I'm a fucking HEDGEHOG?????" Then he left the room and I didn't see him the rest of the night.

The next morning Basil had calmed down enough for me to read the rest of the article (I left out the part about the nicknames). He hid his right paw under him while I read and was more subdued than usual, but at least he wasn't crazed. When we finished I could tell he needed something more.

"Basil," I said. "I'm uncomfortable calling this a flaw or a defect. That would indicate that it impairs you in any way. And since you don't buy gloves (he shot me a look), I think we can just call this an anomaly."

Basil said, "Call it whatever you like. I can't believe I've put this paw up on the window for the whole world to see! The birds and squirrels are probably still talking about it to this day! 'Look at old six toes! Here comes

Frodo! If it isn't Toey the Wonder Cat!! Check out Puss and BOOOOOTS!!'"

I tried to distract him with a joke I remembered: "Hey Basil, do you know how many bones are in the human hand?"

He did not look amused, "No, Carl. I don't"

I replied, "Well, it depends. 27. 28 if I'm lonely."

If you get the joke it is pretty funny. Basil got it, but he didn't laugh. That's when I knew we were in for a long night.

My family of origin, like yours, is full of flaws. But I grew up with two kinds. My mom's sister, my Aunt, was flawed, but she wore her flaws on the outside. She showed them to most everybody. I remember one time being at her house and there was a photo album on a coffee table. I opened it up and there she was, my aunt, the subject of a Polaroid picture taken of her while she was on the toilet! I grew up in a house where the bathroom occupancy was one. Never two. I couldn't believe it. What a heathen! To allow oneself to be photographed on the shitter! But that's who she was. She married a couple of idiots and they were on full display as well.

Now her sister, my mother, was also full of flaws, but she liked to hide hers. Even to this day, doctors and neighbors and family members have no idea what my mom has dealt with. What has consumed her for all of her adult life? My mother's mother introduced her to amphetimines when she was a teenager entering pageants in order to keep the weight off. She was off to the races after that. But she has never been open about it. Not one time. But I thought, growing up, how lucky we were to live in a family where you don't take pictures of people while they're in the bathroom.

As it turns out I had it backwards. Which has been a pretty consistent theme for me. My aunt is happy, in a loving relationship, active, and healthy. I guess flaws on the outside get resolved. Or they're not flaws at all? Maybe anomalies? My mom is dying, lonely, angry, and empty. And that breaks my heart. It didn't have to be this way.

A flaw is defined as an imperfection that detracts from the whole. I guess I just disagree with that. I used to believe that. So I kept my flaws hidden. My father's side of the family went to great lengths to hide their flaws. My grandmother was dead before we knew she was married before my grandfather. And when she wanted to move to the city but her husband didn't, she had the house burned to the ground. While she was at a prayer meeting. So there's that. This is how ingrained this is in me: I hesitate writing about this "secret" even now. It's breaking a rule. That's why I tried to conceal my nicotine addiction for decades. I'm probably only willing to mention that now because I've kicked the habit.

This is my greatest flaw: I try to hide my flaws.

It's interesting. I don't judge others for their "anomalies." Basil is still just as loved today as he was yesterday. I don't see Bumble's flaws or Maggie's flaws. At least they don't detract from the whole. But I have used a completely different measure for myself.

When Basil calmed down and was in a better place he asked, "Carl, is there anything we can do about this?"

I couldn't resist, "I dunno, we could call a Toe Truck??" That began 48 hours of a silent treatment that I fully deserved. I would do it again, though.

23.

The difference between a scar and a wound is time plus treatment.

24.

It's been a few weeks now and Basil has worked through his extra toeness. He told me that he's had that extra digit his whole life and it hadn't bothered him until he realized it was a defect. Which means the only thing that bothered him was he was different than other cats. That's never bothered him before, as he has put it together than other cats don't talk to humans.

So he ended the topic in true Basil form: "Fuck that noise!"

Moving on.

I read where Mel Gibson said to Robert Downey, Jr
(there's a pair I would have liked to hang out with 20
years ago): "It's time to stop hugging the cactus." The
phrase is new to me, but the practice is familiar.

Moving on. I wish I were better at that. Do the thing.
Right or wrong. Learn the lesson. Make the adjustment.
Moving on. If it weren't for my memory and my
imagination I'd actually be trouble free.

That got me thinking about a couple of characters from
the Bible. Judas and Peter. Both betrayed Jesus in the
worst way imaginable. One took his own life, and one
went on to be foundational to the church. The Classic
Church, not the Caucasian republican church. Anyway,
I was wondering what the difference was between the
two? Who could know such things, but it seems that
after the betrayal Judas stopped and Peter kept moving.
And part of the moving on is the understanding that
our identity is not defined by what we do.

There's a great trend in the recovery community, which,
by the way, I am not a part of. Too many people.
Anyway, the term "alcoholic" and "addict" are slowly
fading away. They are being replaced by "person with a
substance use disorder." For decades, people's identities
have been formed by what they do. By their anomalies.
With the new phrase we are acknowledging, first, that
you are a person. Whole and intact. And second, that
you are dealing with an anomaly in which you abuse a
substance. If we are what we do then Basil is an ass
licker. And he's certainly not that. If we are what we do
then I am a thief and a liar. But that's not who I am
either. I am a person who cares for a cat and who

washes dishes and votes in a democracy and is kind to my neighbors.

Basil has been the best Yoda for Mindfulness. For him, the only thing that matters is the present. That doesn't mean he's always this serene creature. He experiences a full range of positive and negative emotions. But he's a cat doing cat things. The extra toe thing? Yeah, that was hard on him. But he's moved past it. Can't really change it. Although I did ask him if he wanted me to ask the vet about getting it removed.

He said, "If I'm going in for plastic surgery I'm getting ass implants first. Basil Thee Cat! I'm the Original Wet Ass Pussy!"

His acceptance of me has really been healing. Mainly because it's not a dumb, blind adoration. If you lock a dog in your trunk for an hour he'll still be glad to see you when you let him out. Basil would bitch slap you for the better part of a day before he's let you off the hook. But he's not trading you in. He knows what we are all capable of.

Moving on.

25.

A memory from a month ago...

Basil is pacing now. And it's my fault. I usually don't watch the news, but when I do I make sure he's napping or otherwise preoccupied. I guess I didn't pay much attention today. The news story, in a nut shell, was this: Cheeto Mussolini wants to send bigger checks. Democrats want to send bigger checks. Republicans want to send bigger checks. Mitch McConnell doesn't want to send bigger checks.

Well, Basil heard that, and now his blood pressure is up, "Mitch McConnell's heart is so black he wouldn't vote for it! That no good, lying, sack of monkey shit giving out a subscription to the Jelly of the Month Club! Where's Cousin Eddie when you need him?? Has anybody tried flipping him on his back??"

I know I said earlier that Basil and I are pretty apolitical. I stand by that statement. But what's going on this year is just stupid. Actually, we don't mind ignorance. What we really oppose, and would be willing to stand in front of a tank for, is ignorance combined with power.

Take Kimball, for example. Kimball is just ignorant. No two ways about it. I don't even know what the current term for him would be, but I'd imagine I've got it wrong. Let's say he is a person with limited intellect? We like Kimball though. I assist with his laundry a little and maybe give him some pointers every once in a while. No problem!

Basil reminded me, "Remember when Kimball brought that hooker home? That was a close call!"

Oh yeah, that was an event! Basil and I were sitting in the living room watching Regis Philbin reruns of Who Wants to Be a Millionaire. We like doing that because now we know the answers and it is fun to pretend we're hearing the questions for the first time.

Regis asked, "Which of the following landlocked countries is entirely contained with another country? Is it: A. Lesotho. B. Burkina Faso. C. Mongolia. D. Luxembourg."

I start shouting, theatrically, "OF COURSE… Lesotho! Only an imbecile doesn't know the answer to this!!"

Basil counters, "WITHOUT question it's Lesotho!! No other option when you think about it!"

Now, the first time we saw this episode neither one of us had ever heard of Lesotho. So we felt as dumb as you do right now. And of course, we both know the only reason we know the answer now is because we've seen the episode six times.

We were in the middle of high fiving ourselves for our geographical prowess when I caught a glimpse of Kimball walking to his apartment with company. Kimball doesn't have company because Kimball doesn't know anybody except us. Plus, he has the social skills of a toddler. And he wears a helmet. His "company" was a female who was dressed rather nicely. Well, not nicely. But she wasn't in sweats.

Basil and I didn't need to see the rerun to know the answer to this one.

Basil acted first, "Go out there before he opens his door and get him in here and leave the hooker outside! If he opens that door he's a good as robbed!"

Now Basil and I don't think that all sex workers are thieves. In fact, we find it funny that in our society we say sex workers "sell their bodies" but people who work in a factory don't. But we knew this sex worker. And in addition to a thief she is also a lousy lay. But what are you going to do? Complain to the manager? Ask for a refund? Well, it looks like Kimball met Betty.

I ran out and shouted for Kimball, "Hey man, get over here, we need to talk to you for a minute!"

Of course he didn't get the hint: "Can it wait?" - He whisper yells - "I've kind of got company here!"

I didn't have much time to come with an excuse, so I blurted out, "Basil is having an allergic reaction and needs your help!"

Any other human would have rolled his eyes and gone about his business. But Kimball loves Basil and usually has his logic coat checked anyway. So he came in and left Betty sitting on a lawn chair by the pool that hasn't been used since Nixon was in office.

"Kimball," I said. "What are you doing??"

"Basil looks fine to me, what's the problem?" Kimball asked.

We didn't have a lot of time because Betty was outside waiting and Kimball has the attention span of a ferret on crystal meth.

"Kimball," I leaned in, "I'm going to shoot straight with you. What you think is about to happen is not going to happen. And then something is going to happen that you haven't considered."

Kimball said, "Well, I think I'm getting ready to have sex with Betty if I can get out of here, and after that I'd imagine she's going home."

"Yeah," I continued. "None of that is happening. Betty is going to charge you for not having sex with her, then she's going to rob you. Here, I'll show you."

I opened the door and saw Betty. Now, Betty and I go back a ways. She and I have never done business together, and she's never robbed me, but I have gotten her out of a jam or two before. And reasoning with Kimball, who was even more distracted than normal, was going nowhere.

"Hey Betty," I shouted and gestured for her to come over. "This is Kimball and he's my friend. Also, you should know that Kimball's attic is a little dusty."

Kimball piped in, "Carl, you know my apartment is only one story!"

Betty and I exchanged a look. Betty was a hooker and a thief, but she didn't want trouble. And attention usually brought trouble.

Betty looked down at her wrist where a watch would have been and said, "Hey Kimball, I just forgot. I've got somewhere to be."

And she was gone.

Kimball said, "Well shit. There goes my new girlfriend. I'm off to the cold shower then."

Sorry for the detour. We like Kimball. And Betty. We don't have an issue with impotent ignorance, and I mean that in the best possible way. What Basil and I hate is ignorant people in power. It's the power part that allow their ignorance to hurt others. Ignorant people who have access to power always hurt the innocent. You can't possibly come up with an exception. So here's some ignorance for you. The current party in power represents that they are pro-life. Over 300,000 people dead because the current administration didn't manage the pandemic. Is that pro-life? Oh, by the way. The very politicians that mocked the virus as a hoax have lined up in front of healthcare workers to receive a vaccine that was developed through stem cell research, which pro-life folks oppose (unless it personally benefits you). You'll pass on a stimulus package to serve your political interests when there are thousands of people who are food insecure and literally on the brink of giving up. You will use tear gas on nonviolent US citizens so someone can get a picture of you holding a Bible upside down in front of a church you don't go to.

But that's not even the pinnacle. I don't even need to tell the story. If you want the greatest modern example of empowered buffoonery I only have to say three words: Four Seasons Landscaping. Your honor, I rest my case. If you don't know the story, let Google be your friend on this one.

Basil chimes in, "Don't forget Rudy's hair leaking!!! Or Rudy on Borat!!! Or just Rudy!!"

These people aren't Republicans. I actually haven't seen a Republican in a few years. Trump supporters aren't Republicans. And any decent Republican is hiding out right now. Biden will bring this to the table: The real

Republicans can come out of hiding again. We like them as much as the Democrats. And the Libertarians. Let's not forget them.

But you can keep the Mitch McConnell's of the world. I ought to send Betty over there to see if she could cheer him up a little. I'll keep an eye on his helmet for him.

26.

I was in the back of the diner, making dirty dishes clean, minding my own business, when I heard the one phrase that always makes me freeze in my tracks. Instant paralysis.

"Hey, Carl!"

I knew it wasn't the boss or Bumble. I knew it wasn't anybody I had regular contact with. I was gripped with fear. I unfroze myself and made my way to door to the dining area. I peered around the corner, cautiously. Only to see two guys I've never seen before seated at the counter. One of them was named Carl. Maybe it was Karl. Who the fuck knows. But they weren't yelling for me. What an exhale!

First off, I'm not in a witness protection program. Also, I'm not hiding from anybody. Well, not really. I guess the only person I'm hiding from is myself. My life has been long enough and complicated enough that, depending on who might recognize me, I might be greeted with an embrace or a 9mm. Truthfully, I'd be deserving of either.

A reputation is a funny thing. My grandmother on my dad's side used to tell me, "All you have is your good name." Yeah, the same one who hid her previous marriage and burned the family house down because she wanted to be closer to the Piggy Wiggly. Again, she didn't actually burn the house down. She hired it out. That's hilarious to me to think about. She was a little, white haired, quiet, unassuming, polite elderly woman. Active in the church and in the ladies auxiliary. Pillar of the community. I would love to have a transcript of her hiring the hit on her house.

I'd imagine she talked to one of the Mays boys from Hi Hat. Maybe Willie or Wilbur. Not a shade of difference between the two. But they had a reputation. And so did my grandmother. And maintaining their respective reputations would require that one not be seen with the other. So I can't imagine how they arranged to meet, and then, what took place in the meeting. To be clear, I'm not judging my grandmother for having her own house burned down. She knew what she wanted and usually got it. It's the secret of it that was handed down that I've had to undo. She was a bad bitch, in the best way, but pretended to be innocent. And members of her family that were not as adept as her in keeping their flaws hidden were cut off at the knees. Never spoke of again. Her husband had a brother who drank too much. And he did it in the daylight in the front yard on a Sunday. Not even the back yard. Once that became known he was not allowed in the family home ever again. Their son, my father, had only seen his uncle a couple of times, and then, at a distance. He was used as an object lesson for how not to live your life. If my grandfather ever had any communication with his brother he had to do it secretly.

It's almost as if there existed a rule which stated: "If a tree falls in the forest and no one sees it, it didn't actually fall."

When you think about it, the word "reputation" literally means "what other people think about you." So one minute you're the beloved Ellen, the happy, gay, benevolent, dancing, adored queen of daytime TV. THEN people start talking about what a hard ass you are. But really, who's not a hard ass in the comfort of their own space? The tide turns, and now her reputation is tarnished. But she can (and has) come back from that. Basil likes her, and he's a wicked judge of character. Basil wants Ellen to be president and Jimmy Fallon to be vice president. Basil said if that ever happened in his lifetime he'd be forced to walk around with a permanent boner.

So when you're reputation is ruined I guess you have a couple options. Maybe three. One is to try to repair the damage. That's a pretty long list when you think about it. Bill Clinton went from an UDBBBJ (under the desk bare back blowjob) back to mostly a statesman. He's pretty welcome in public. Martha Stuart is one of my favorite comeback stories. From the Gray Bar hotel to Snoop's side piece. Well, not that kind of side piece. But she made it back. George W. made it back and didn't even try. He just stood next to Cheeto and George W.'s stock went through the roof. I'd imagine Lori Laughlin will make a nice comeback. Hugh Grant made it back after his date with Estella Thompson (you might remember her as Divine Brown). She didn't do badly either after that date, raking in over a million dollars in publicity deals.

Louis CK made it back, kind of. He has this stand up bit where he laments that everybody has a thing or two they like sexually, but they get to express that in the privacy of their own homes. And for most people not named Kardashian, that stays private. He says now the whole civilized world knows what his kink is. I said he kind of made it back because I still didn't want to know what his was.

But then there's some that try but didn't make it back. Bill Cosby. Harvey Weinstein. Jeffrey Epstein (who didn't kill himself). Haven't heard from Matt Lauer in a while. And OJ absolutely, without question, allegedly, killed his wife. He's not coming back.

Garrison Keillor hasn't made it back and that makes me sad. He was like a family member to me. I used to love his radio show. For months after he was fired (#metoo) we all thought it was because he touched a woman on her back. At least that's what he owned up to. That was the initial report. Turns out he's just a horny little Lutheran. Allegedly. Not helping his case, his response to the controversy in 2019 was to encourage people to "lighten up." It seems the key to not making it back would be not owning your shit. Right, Pete Rose? I'm talking about you!

And then there's people like me. I'm a mixed bag. I didn't kill my wife, and I didn't get an UDBBBJ from an intern. I was offered a BBBJ from two toothless streetwalkers once. After I declined their offer we had a fantastic conversation on a park bench. But I'm no angel.

Woody Harrelson plays Vince Boudreau in the 1999 film, Play It to the Bone. Here's a quote from Vince in the movie: "If a man builds a thousand bridges and sucks one dick they don't call him a bridge builder, they call him a cocksucker."

That's the sort of homophobic horseshit that was acceptable last century. Hopefully, we have evolved beyond that now. A better equivalent comes to mind.

I knew a guy once that claimed to have had sex with sheep. And since "sheep" is both the singular and plural of the word, I don't know if it was a 'one off' or a regular thing. And if it was a regular thing, I don't know if it was one particular sheep or if he had multiple partners. So many unanswered questions. But I remember that guy's name. And I've forgotten a thousand names since.

So maybe Vince was right. That guy could have invented the next vaccine, but I'll only remember him for one thing.

So it seems that bad deeds might outweigh good ones? Who knows? The bad deeds of others make better headlines. For those of us who have ruined our reputations to one degree or another, we can either be crushed by the weight, wade through the mire for a comeback, or just leave town.

Of all the people who have had a hard time in pop culture, I miss Michael Richards the most. Kramer was such an iconic role. After his banana peel moment it seemed like it just consumed him. Jerry had him on his show a few years later, the Cars and Coffee one. That just broke my heart. You could see that it still defined him. He couldn't let it go. Of course what he said was wrong. It was vile, but that separates him from the rest of humanity only in that it became known and it wasn't a secret. Hidden and Known are the only two delineations one can make in human error. Maybe severity. Maybe.

One of Basil's favorite jokes: A guy walks up to a woman at the bar and says, "Will you sleep with me for a million dollars?"

She looks the guy over and says, "Yes, for a million dollars I will."

The guy responds, "What about for twenty dollars?"

She replies angrily, "What, exactly, do you think I am?"

He calmly replies, "We've already established what you are, now we're just talking price."

So maybe severity comes into play, maybe not.

My answer was to leave town. To not suffocate under the weight. To not fight my way back either. This seemed like to most "water" thing to do. I'm occasionally trying to be like water. To just flow, to not resist.

I know this is true: Once I ruined my reputation I was able to live more free than I ever have in my entire life. Not that I recommend my particular path. In fact, I'd avoid it if you have the choice.

27.

Roland taught me this: In some respects, to some extent, absolute certainty frequently proceeds extreme emotions such as anger and despair. Not only is there great freedom in not needing to be right about anything, but the ease of uncertainty, if embraced, can be a balm to the soul.

I wonder how many internal and interpersonal conflicts would have been eased if absolute certainty were not embraced.

It seems to Basil and I that our culture has started valuing opinion and feeling over facts. "Fake News," as it turns out, is better described as "Unfavorable News."

Basil reminded me of some of his favorite quotes:
Abraham Lincoln: "While you're trying to figure out
who's right can y'all try to be nice to each other for
fuck's sake?" Followed by the Lee Harvey Oswald
classic, "You miss 100% of the shots you don't take."
Another Lincoln quote Basil likes: "But we already
bought the tickets."

You don't think those are accurate quotes? Fight me.

28.

Roland stopped by today. That's always a treat for Basil and me. He's the only person on the planet that is allowed to just walk in whenever he wants. He's family for us. I met him my first week out here, even before Basil. Roland and I met by chance, but in a short conversation at the grocery store I knew I needed this man in my life. I wasn't wrong about that.

Roland is also the only person on earth that makes Basil sit still and shut up. Basil's favorite activity is to talk shit when company is over, since no one can understand him. But when Roland comes over, Basil just sits at his feet and listens. Roland has, I don't know, I guess I'd call it an aura? That sounds kind of mystical, but it's actually a math equation. Years plus pain plus observation plus curiosity = Roland. One of the things that's different about him than others of a certain age is he is energetic and playful. Curious, even. I don't know exactly how old he is, but he's been getting discount coffee at McDonald's for about 25 years now. You know that tired look that you see in seniors? Bent by the years of opposing wind, some bear the resemblance of blown over grass. Not Roland. Better posture than people half his age, he greets my words with wonder and curiosity. In a word, he's vibrant. He's also a badass.

When Roland comes over, Basil and I feel like we're plugged into some kind of power source. So we just sit and soak.

Roland has just come back from a yoga class. With his girlfriend. Who is also vibrant and beautiful. But when he is with us he is fully with us. I guess that's what we like about him. He had every reason to be thinking a little about last night, earlier today, or what was coming up later. But while he is with us, we are the center of the universe. He's been teaching me how to do that (Be mindful) for a while now. If I had met him as a young man I could have skipped some hard lessons. But when I tell him that he says that we met when we were supposed to meet. He's the one who's teaching me how to be like water.

The only time I've seen him angry was when I wasn't being kind to myself. It was almost as if there were two of me, and he was pissed at the one who was being abusive to the other one of me. As I write that out it makes sense to me, but I wonder if you follow me? He was able to be angry with the part of me that was self-harming. Is that better? It was such a unique experience for me. I've traditionally not handled angry people well. It's usually fight or flight. But his anger was kind and corrective. Maybe it can't be described accurately. I know my time with him has helped me survive myself.

29.

It was a random Tuesday night and I'm just relaxing, reading a few chapters from Roland's book (you didn't think a guy that awesome hadn't written a book did you?) and Basil calls out from the other room: "Hey Carl, you ever have a sharp, shooting pain across your chest, like someone's got a voodoo doll of you and they're stabbing it?"

"No Basil," I shouted. "I don't think so."

A minute or two goes by.

"How about now?"

30.

When I wake in the middle of the night I sometimes still reach out for her. I remember who she used to be, before she changed. As Roland has taught me, it's not absolutely certain what took her from me. I have suspects. But it could have been anything, really. One of my least favorite phrases in medicine: Idiopathic. No known cause.

I've got a picture from before that I look at frequently. She's standing in front of a mirror, fixing her hair after I had just done my damnedest to mess it up. She's wearing jeans, a bra, and looking amazing. But it's something else that draws me back to the picture. It's the look on her face. It's a mix of lightning and contentment. I've seen the look on a lion as she devours her prey. Who was the predator and who was the prey that day could be debated. But in that picture she looked pretty proud of herself. As she should have been.

I had the time that I had, and I'm thankful for that. But grief still visits regularly. I try to turn the grief into good nostalgia. She loved the beach and I went into no small debt to make sure she got her toes in the sand a couple of times a year. It was worth every penny. Tennyson was exactly, painfully right. It was far better to have loved than to have never known.

31.

Basil and I are watching Lion King tonight on a VCR. How we wound up with the VCR and the tape is a story too long and convoluted, so let's just say we have it and leave it at that.

Hell, might as well tell it. I don't have anywhere to be at the moment.

Frankie, the boss at the diner, came up to me one day in the back and said, "Hey Carl, Bumble tells me you used to be a counselor or something like that."

(Reminder: Tell Bumble to keep her damn mouth shut.)

"No," I lied. "I don't know where she got that."

Frankie persisted, "Anyway, suppose I run something by you?"

I was pretty clear, ""Frankie, if there's a dish that needs washed, let me know. Otherwise, kiss my ass."

I can tell Frankie to 'kiss my ass' because I'm a good dishwasher who's never missed a shift. That puts me in rare air.

But Frankie wasn't hearing me. "Carl, here's the thing. No matter what I do I can't get my wife to…"

I interrupted Frankie, "Stop. Seriously. I don't have any idea how to get your wife to do anything!"
Frankie kept on, louder this time, "I can't get her to quit drinking! Every night she's at least half in the bag! Carl, it's killing me!"

Frankie thought about it a minute, then he said, "Carl, I'll pay you. Anything!"

"Frankie," I began, "I can't take payment, I don't have a license to practice. But as a friend I can suggest something."

"Anything!" Frankie exclaimed.

I said, "Be a better husband. Be nicer. Be cleaner. Cook more. Watch her shows. Rub her feet. Talk nice about her mother."

He said, "You really think that will make her stop?"

I continued, "No Frankie. That's not going to make her stop. But it will make you a better person, and when you're thinking about it later, you'll know you did everything you could. She'll stop when she decides to stop. And it has nothing to do with you. Stop trying to control her. You can't."

Frankie actually looked a little relieved. He reached in his pocket for his wallet and I held up my hand to stop him. That's when he hurried back to the storage closet and brought back a VCR.

"Here, take this," he said. "I don't need it anymore. Consider it a bonus for never missing work."
So that's how Basil and I got a VCR. The library had a copy of the Lion King, so now we're caught up. Back to the Lion King.

It's one of my favorite movies. Good songs. Funny. Insightful. A good villain.

I'd seen the movie before, but I got to be with Basil the first time he saw it. He was no stranger to Disney and knew the rough formula that made the franchise great. The movie comes up to the part where Scar says, sending Mufasa to his grave, "Long live the king!" Basil just falls over on the couch. Kind of like I did when Ned Stark didn't make it in GoT. I paused the tape and waited for Basil to come back to Earth.

He kind of shook his head and asked, "Dream sequence?" Nope. "Coma?" No. "MUFASA'S DEAD???"

"Yes," I said. "Basil. He's dead."

Basil hissed, "That Scar's a little bitch. If he doesn't get some karma from this I'm burning the tape!"

We watch the rest of the movie. Then it becomes strangely quiet. Basil and I are usually quite comfortable in silence. But this is different. Basil is shook. Something is different.

"So Simba..," Basil begins. "Quite a life, huh? How long do you think he was in exile?"

"Well," I said. "A few years? Maybe three or so?"
Basil seems unusually thoughtful right now.

Basil asked, "Carl, are you in exile?"

I wept for the first time in a long time. I couldn't stop it. It's like that word opened something up in me.

First off, Basil rarely uses my name. When he does, it signals anger or thoughtfulness. Frankly, I prefer the anger. Thoughtfulness toward me has always been uncomfortable. I think because it goes against my narrative.

After I pull myself together it's clear he's waiting for an answer. "No Basil, I'm not in exile. I'm in Elko. They're miles apart."

Basil said, "Nice deflection Carl. Seriously, are you in exile?"

I just stared back at him. I didn't know what to say.

Basil went on to talk about Simba, and how Simba spent years blaming himself for his father's death. And how that lack of forgiveness kept Simba away from Pride Rock and his rightful inheritance. Plus, it allowed that son of a bitch Scar to keep his illegitimate rule. And if it hadn't been for the ghost of Mufasa, Simba would have stayed in exile.

Basil asked, "Any of this sounding familiar? Carl?"

Now I'm getting annoyed. Which is an emotion I'd do fine without. Wouldn't miss it at all. I prefer Basil the Smart Ass or Basil the Grouch or Basil the Sleepy. Or grumpy. Any of the dwarfs except for Basil the Thoughtful.

I'm Carl the Dishwasher. That's all. Nothing before. No exile.

Basil continued, "Carl, I watch you look at the ground when you talk to people. I watch you brush by mirrors. I watch you change the subject when you become the subject. I hear you shout in the night sometimes. Do you know what you scream? Every time it's 'I'm sorry.' Every single time. Not once have you shouted, 'Just like that, Margot!' You're always sorry. Always apologizing. The other day when Kimball said he stopped by but you weren't home. You told him you were sorry. For not being home? For not anticipating when he was going to come over? WHAT WERE YOU SORRY FOR CARL??

"You're always telling people to be good to themselves. But you live in a prison made of walls you constructed.

Out of imaginary bricks. What are you sorry for? Tell me!"

I was almost speechless. I hate this. But I guess I owed him an answer. "Basil, I let a lot of people down."

Basil looked at me, "And?"

I replied, "And it was wrong. And they got hurt."

Basil asked me, "And what did they do when you hurt them? Carl?"

I thought about that for a minute. "Well, I guess some of them walked away, as they should have."

Basil corrected me, "You mean they discarded you."

I said, "Sure, they discarded me, as I deserved."

Basil said, "You seem pretty sure that the discarding was appropriate. Have you thought about that? Because you don't seem to do that to other people. You don't seem to do that to me. Remember that night I shit on your pillow because you wouldn't give me a bite of your tuna? I'm still here. Remember when you left the charcoal pencil out and I drew cat whiskers on you and you didn't see it before you got to work? You threw a shoe at me, but I'm still here.

"The thing is, Carl, if you treated others the way you treat yourself, you'd be a real asshole. We're all a mixed bag. Some good, some not so good. We're all capable of all of it. Sainthood and the Jail, depending on the day and the circumstances."

I interrupted, "OK, Basil. Thanks for sharing with me."

Basil shot back, "Carl, you're not going to dismiss this. How do you know I'm not Mufasa's ghost and this is your turning point? Maybe I'm the cosmic messenger to announce the day you let yourself out of exile? That's not too far-fetched, given that I'm a fucking cat and I'm talking to you right now!

"Carl, what happened back then is a story you told yourself about events that you only know something about. Pretty shaky ground if you ask me. And even if you're right about how things went down, even if you were way out of bounds, who says that's an indictment about WHO you are? Since when does what we do signal who we are? I lick my ass, Carl. Am I an ass licker?"

When he asked me that, something started to lift a little. I felt a few of the rocks I carry in my backpack slip to the floor. He's right about one thing, I have had a tendency to blur the lines between what I have done and who I am. Also, I can't believe I'm having a serious conversation with a cat. When we're laughing or breaking balls it seems just a little more normal? Maybe not to you, but to me it does. But this is some deep shit we're into. I'm going to have to pay him if he keeps going. Thankfully, he's about done.

Basil leaned back on the couch, "Carl, you're a good guy. You've done some dumb shit in your life. Get down off the cross and stop treating yourself like you're the Zodiac killer. You're not the Zodiac killer, are you Carl?"

"No."

"Then Hakuna Matata, bitch! Let's watch a Bruce Willis movie. No chance of a life lesson in any of those. I want to see someone blow some shit up."

32.

I regret taking something that wasn't mine far more than not taking what was owed to me.

33.

When I packed up my old, rusted CRV to come out West I also made room for plenty of shame and guilt. Somehow, those got wedged in between the boxes. You'd think I would have noticed the shame, given its foul, rotting smell.

Shame is a voice. It is said to you by you. No one can "shame" you. Maybe you have heard a phrase that is pretty familiar: "Shame on you." Shame is something that can rest on you, for sure, but it's a garment that we dress ourselves in. The garment is made of rotting flesh. More accurately, old rotting flesh. Because shame is always rooted in the past. Bones dug up from long ago deeds. The garment's one purpose is to evaluate your worth. And there's always one answer: "You aren't worth shit." The Garment takes stock of you, measures you for cost and benefit. The Garment types some numbers into a calculator and tears off the paper at the end. It's longer than a receipt from CVS. The Garment squints at the numbers and exclaims, "We can throw this one in the land fill."

You might squeak out a reply, "Maybe the recycle bin? Or Good Will?"

The Garment sneers, "Nothing but trash here."

I suspect many people are draped in The Garment when they take their own lives. It's the only garment that makes one colder the thicker it is.

The scaffolding that is up inside me is designed to exfoliate the old, rotting flesh of shame. I can live with the guilt. The guilt helps me change and provides hope. Even the good pain of a bad choice is instructive. You can tell whether or not you're dealing with guilt or shame by the conclusion you come to. If its shame, the conclusion is you're worthless so why even try? If it's guilt, then you'll be motivated to try again, to be better.

Shame almost killed me, but Guilt brought me to Elko. What an oasis!

34.

The guilt, then. Maybe I should talk about that. That's a long list. I just typed it out, then backspaced the whole damn thing. Steak and Eggs is the difference between a contribution and a sacrifice. I'm not trying to lay it all out here.

But I will tell you about the last thing. The straw, as it were.

I was a helper back East. I was mostly, exactly that. I liked helping people. I actually liked it too much. My worth got caught up in it. I felt like I mattered because of who I helped. I imagined a picnic when I died, attended by the people that I had helped. It wasn't later that I realized this picnic daydream was there to fill the void of how I was supposed to feel about myself on my own. I never verbalized it, but I thought if I helped a lot of people then I must be worth something.

So I wasn't a really a helper, but more of a helper*. Don't go looking at the bottom of the page. The asterisk is there to just let you know that I know I'm complicated.

Her mother called and said her daughter was in the ER. The family had come up on the hard side of the mountain. They scraped for all of it. The daughter was pregnant and the dad was a piece of shit. He was abusive, but she would always take him back. He had multiple girlfriends, but she always forgave. He wouldn't work, but she always supported.

I had known the whole family for some time. So when the mom called and asked me to come to the hospital, I did so without hesitation. My training said not to go. My training was right. But when asked for help, I would frequently ignore my training in favor of helping, but not for the right reasons.

When I arrived at the ER, I found out that the piece of shit boyfriend, in a drunken rage, had kicked his girlfriend in the stomach until she passed out. Because dinner wasn't ready when he wanted it. She lost the baby as a result.

The police asked the family where to find the boyfriend. They were pretty tight lipped about it. The police had not been friends of the family before, so their suspicion was warranted. They tended to handle matters themselves.

But I had a pretty good idea where he would be. Now, this is point where I left Reason Island. What I did next has been viewed as positive by many who have heard the story. But it wasn't. What I did next was neither brave nor honorable. What I did next was from an unwell place.

I went to where I thought he might be. My whole body was shaking with rage. Every muscle in my body was tense. Second floor of an apartment complex on the East end. I knocked on the door. He cracked it, and when he saw it was me he opened the door further. Because I'm a helper. I'm safe.

I told him this lie: "I've called the police and told them where you are; they're on their way now. I'm here to keep you here until they arrive."

I told him this, hoping he would strike first, somehow justifying what I would do next. And I was right. He tried to get past me, and that's all I needed. When the fury was over, he laid in a crumpled bloodied heap on the floor. What kept me from killing him, I'm still perplexed about that. I left and called 911 and told them where to find him.

I went home and I waited. It wasn't long before a cruiser came to pick me up. I knew I was in trouble and I knew I wasn't going to be a helper anymore. I was pretty OK with both of those things.

I had a good lawyer, someone I had helped before. That, and the "extenuating circumstances" worked in my favor to avoid prison. The "extenuating circumstances" were that everybody from the prosecution to the judge hated that guy. So they took it easy on me. Even the cop that arrested me said he wished he'd had a bucket of popcorn to watch the show. The state thought it was a good idea for me to take a 30 day time out, and then my probation officer helped me get my probation transferred to Nevada.

I was wrong. It was not my responsibility to punish him. It was arrogant of me to think so. It was disordered of me to think so. My crime in the matter has always been overshadowed and minimized because the guy was a monumental asshole. Which he was. And is. But it was not my punishment to give. And it's probably a miracle that I didn't kill him. I can tell you this, I wasn't trying not to. He was in the hospital for 14 days and will he always have to deal with the consequences of my behavior.

So now you know the back story of how I got to Nevada. And you also know the backdrop for my recurring nightmare. About once a week, in my dream, I walk through a door. It can be any door. An office, the diner, a random business, even an airplane. And when I pass through the threshold, seated in the floor in front of me is the guy. Bloodied and swollen from my hands and the baseball bat that was behind his door. And surrounding him are a dozen other people I have hurt in my life. Not like this guy, but in other ways. In some cases, in more severe ways. And they're silent. And they stare up at me, and it's obvious to me in the dream that they are waiting for me to say something. Or do something. They are anticipating, based on what I do next, to experience a soothing of the pain I created. And then I freeze. I cannot move, and I cannot speak. I can't even breathe. The only thing I can do is see people in pain that I caused look at me with the additional disappointment of me not being able to help them now. I can't move closer to help. I can't speak to offer an apology. Even the face I'm making looks like apathy, but that's not what I am feeling. I feel as if I am on fire. Burning from the inside out. Like trash in a barrel.

That's why I make dirty dishes clean. That's why I'm not a helper anymore. You can't be a helper when you are the source of the pain. "I'm sorry" just isn't enough. It's not even close. The last gift I had to give was my absence.

35.

It's a music night. Music is how I illustrate time. The TV is off. Basil and I have dinner and then I sit down at the little keyboard I bought at a pawn shop out here. It's not much, but we're pretty easy to please. So music night is part discussion, part listening. Basil and I will discuss songs and artists. And then we'll play some songs on the computer and I'll accompany.

He and I have pretty similar tastes in music. We both love James Taylor and Lyle Lovett. We both love Harry Styles and Ray Lamontagne. We're Elvis people. We tolerate the Beatles. We think Chris Stapleton and Justin Timberlake make an amazing duo and we're pretty certain that Bruno Mars and H.E.R. are both musical savants.

We have our differences, though. And they're stark. Basil likes Jim Morrison and the Doors. I actually don't know anyone who likes Jim Morrison aside from Basil. And Basil's favorite song right now is Small Worlds by Mac Miller. Mr. Miller is no longer with us so, out of respect, I'll just say I don't care for the song. Basil likes Whitesnake and I don't. But Basil doesn't like them for their music, he likes them for their music videos. Specifically, their music video, "Here I Go Again." Basil has a crush on Tawny Kitaen. After he saw that video he became obsessed for a while. He once told me he'd like to make her wish she'd been born a cat. Which I thought was a little extreme. And an unwelcome visual.

I came home one day and found him watching Tawny in The Perils of Gwendoline in the Land of the Yik-Yak. Yes, that is a movie. No, I do not recommend it. He was mesmerized. After it was over he asked me, "You got a cigarette?"

I really dig George Benson, Earl Klugh, and Bob James. Basil, not so much. I can spend some quality time with Flim and the BB's. They were one of the first bands to record their musical digitally. Jimmy (Flim), Bill Berg (B), and Billy Barber (B). Bass, percussion and keys. Give a listen to their album, Tricycle. See if you agree with me or Basil.

So we do that for a while. Argue. Listen. Play. Repeat. And then, at the end, when we're tired, I play Basil something. It's not a song. It's never a song. But is it music? Kind of. There's no form to it. No identifiable chord progression or key or tempo or time signature. Have you ever written free verse on paper? Just writing.

No punctuation. No theme. Just writing. It's interesting what comes out when you do that. Well, this is like that, except on a keyboard. I've been doing it for years, and I can tell whether or not we are going to be close friends depending on whether or not you track with me on this.

The truth is there aren't enough words in the English language to convey the depths of human emotion. That's why music exists in the first place. It really makes me sad to think about people who can't get a goose bump. Who can't be transported into another universe through music.

And so, we end on a sort of piece of music without guardrails. It's over when it's over.

On this particular night, after the music ended, we just sat together. Quiet.

When we first started music night Basil was a little jealous because he can't play an instrument. Well, he could, but he just hasn't found the right one yet. Also, when we first started, I wasn't really comfortable playing music in front of him. I feel that way generally about most people.

So this particular night, we're sitting there together and Basil asks me, "You played a different chord tonight. Toward the end. What was it? That was an interesting way to end a piece."

Basil is learning some music as we go. Not that I know a lot of theory, but just enough. So I thought about it, and tried to remember where the wandering piece went. I couldn't think of it.

Then Basil said, "Actually, it was the last chord you played. What was that?"

Now I remembered. It was a Cmaj7 chord. It's C, E, G, B. If you know a little about music, you recognize a basic C chord: C,E,G. The maj7 is the B at the end. So I played it for Basil.

"That's it!" he said. "Hey, tell me something. It felt like there was supposed to be another chord after that, but you ended it on that C 7 thing."

Basil is certainly developing an ear. I told him what he heard was what we call dissonance. The C at the bottom and the B at the top are arguing with each other. There's unresolved tension.

Basil said, "Then I like dissonance!"

"I'm learning to like dissonance," I replied. "Actually it's one of the things you've taught me, Basil. When we first met I wanted a resolution to every tension as fast as possible. But you sometimes seek out tension. You don't resolve conflict, you manage it."

Basil is pretty uncomfortable being complimented. And I'm pretty uncomfortable complimenting a cat for giving me a life lesson. So we just sat for a minute and stared at each other.

"Play the song again," he said. "And don't resolve it again. Dissonance is beautiful."

"I told him, "I'm not sure if I can remember it."

Basil said, "Either play the damn thing or we're listening to the Doors!"

"As you wish."

Ten minutes later, after more free form music, Basil seems satisfied. So am I. Neither one of us know what the story was about, but we like how it ended.

36.

Basil and I were sitting in front of the TV in silence, watching a mob of angry white guys, a few white girls, and a few people of color (who were obviously lost) storm the Capitol. They were streaming into the rotunda, acting like they were in a fraternity at Faber College and had just broken into Dean Wormer's house. Look at the picture of the guy holding the lectern wearing a stocking hat and tell me I'm wrong.

Basil said, "Well, now we've got a simpler definition of White privilege: "If you break into the Capitol of the United States and start waving a confederate flag and you're not immediately shot, you've just experienced White privilege."

One of the Gravy Seals that stormed the sacred space ended up tazing himself in the testicles and dying from the ensuing heart attack. He may or may not have been trying to steal a portrait of Tip O'Neill. Allegedly.

Basil said, "Man, I'm glad I'm not white! How do you taze yourself in the balls? Logistically, I mean? Like, what was the intent? Why did he have a tazer? Who was he intending to taze? And how did he mistake his intended target for his nut sack? And how did he make it that far into the Capitol with what must be a fairly low level of intelligence in the first place? Allegedly."

"You're not white?" I asked. I'd never thought about it, really.

"Carl," Basil began dryly, "Cats have breeds, not races. Do you want me to go get Kimball's helmet for you?"

I'm listening to Basil, but I'm also entertaining myself thinking about this guy walking (gingerly) up to the pearly gates and meeting St. Peter. I wonder if, when we get to heaven, there's various lines we have to get in. Kind of like when you go to a convention and they have you get in line based on your last name. But instead, you get in line based on how you died. You walk through the door and you see various groups of people huddled together, working through a queue. With signs overhead. There's the Cardiac line. The Overdose line. There's a line for fireworks. One for car accidents. There's even a Choking on Steak at a Restaurant sign. One for Skydiving and one for Hunger. Thousands of signs, and people in every line. Except one. The sign reads: Death by Testicle Tazing. There's only one guy in that line, and everybody in the grand hall is whispering at that guy. Snickering. Somebody mumbles the joke: "Shocking!" Even the guy who dropped the safe on his own head is relieved. There's two people in his line.

There are 150 people in the line that reads, "Coconut to the Head." That's an actual statistic. 150 annual deaths by a coconut falling.

In fact, there's only one other line containing a single person. The sign reads, "Speared by a Swordfish." There you'll find Randy Llanes, commercial fisherman and all around great guy. He took a chance on a swordfish and speared it and the fish returned the favor. Even Randy is chuckling at the Testicle Tazing guy, "At least I died in battle!"

This guy, Mr. Electric Balls, died in support of a president who told him to take back the Capitol. The president who is known to his followers as a champion to the unborn. Despite his extensive and consistent record of how he treats people who have been born.

Basil sums it up for me, "It's a fucking cult. No different than Jonestown. All we're missing is the Kool Aid."

As of this writing, the news anchors are mentioning possible impeachment or invoking the 25th Amendment. Basil and I can't wait for him to be gone so we can get back to incompetent politicians as opposed to dangerous dictators.

37.

After work last night I stopped by the quik mart to get a Slim Jim, Twizzlers, and an orange soda. Don't judge. I wanted vodka and a blunt. So I made the healthier choice. I could have had a V8 and a wheatgrass smoothie. Yoga and a prayer? But I was angry. If you do yoga when you're angry you're likely to blow an O ring. What was I angry about? Couldn't tell you. Really, that's the truth. I mean, I've got a running list like most people. But I couldn't put my finger on what I was sideways about. So when I went into the quik mart I was a little salty. I should have had a warning label.

When I walked in everything seemed just like I left it. Same merchandise. Bobby behind the counter, just like most days. Bobby isn't interested in conversation or customer satisfaction. Which suits me just fine. Most days I'd rather not talk and I sure don't need Bobby making sure I'm happy.

I went over by the Twizzlers and I saw something new. A shelf. Containing items from throughout the store. Below the items was a sign. It said, "Clarence." I stared at it for a minute. Yup, I read it right. Looks like the quik mart was getting rid of some "Clearance" items, and Bobby misspelled the word.

"Hey Bobby, is Clarence here?" I asked.
Bobby looked confused, "Carl, I don't know nobody named Clarence."

I continued, "Well, I'd like to talk to him if he comes in. Would you give him my number if you see him?"

Bobby sounded a little irritated, "Carl, I don't know a Clarence, how will I know to give him your number?"

"Bobby, I'd like to talk to him about buying some of his stuff," I said, gesturing to the shelf.

You could see a small lightbulb go off in his small head, "Oh, you're looking at the Clarence shelf!"

"Whatever you say, Bobby. How's a guy get his own shelf in here anyway? I've got some canned goods I wouldn't mind getting rid of."

Now Bobby is clenching his teeth, "CARL! Those items are CLARENCE!!"

I'm shouting back, "I KNOW, AND WHEN HE COMES IN ASK HIM TO GIVE ME A CALL! I WANT TO BUY THOSE SALTINES FROM HIM!"

Bobby's face was beet red as he turned around and went to the back, slamming items on the shelves as he went. He didn't come back out so I shouted, "Bobby, can you check me out up here?"

I heard him shout from the back, "Take it. On the house!"

So that's how I got free Slim Jims, Twizzlers, and Orange Soda AND a good bit of entertainment for free. I didn't need that Vodka after all.

The next morning Basil and I settled in for a rare event. It was inauguration day and Joe and Kamala were getting sworn in and The Orange One was loading the U'Haul. Basil and I are looking forward to politics being boring again. Hopefully. He and I are glad to see Joe and Kamala, although neither one of us want to go out and get a Biden/Harris flag.

I was unusually moved during the inauguration. It is true that I welcomed the change in administrations. Also true that I thought the previous administration was run by idiots. Hateful idiots. But not so much that I would feel tears welling up. Basil and I were both silent during the ceremony, which was very unusual.

Then something amazing happened. Amanda Gorman, a young poet, took the stage and shared a poem she wrote for the inauguration. The power of that poem,

filled with wisdom and insight, left Basil and I in a
knotted up mess. It was titled "The Hill We Climb." I
wanted you to read it. Here's what she said:

"When day comes we ask ourselves,
where can we find light in this never-ending shade?
The loss we carry,
a sea we must wade
We've braved the belly of the beast
We've learned that quiet isn't always peace
And the norms and notions
of what just is
Isn't always just-ice
And yet the dawn is ours
before we knew it
Somehow we do it
Somehow we've weathered and witnessed
a nation that isn't broken
but simply unfinished
We the successors of a country and a time
Where a skinny Black girl
descended from slaves and raised by a single mother
can dream of becoming president
only to find herself reciting for one
And yes we are far from polished
far from pristine
but that doesn't mean we are
striving to form a union that is perfect
We are striving to forge a union with purpose
To compose a country committed to all cultures, colors,
characters and
conditions of man
And so we lift our gazes not to what stands between us
but what stands before us

We close the divide because we know, to put our future
first,
we must first put our differences aside
We lay down our arms
so we can reach out our arms
to one another
We seek harm to none and harmony for all
Let the globe, if nothing else, say this is true:
That even as we grieved, we grew
That even as we hurt, we hoped
That even as we tired, we tried
That we'll forever be tied together, victorious
Not because we will never again know defeat
but because we will never again sow division
Scripture tells us to envision
that everyone shall sit under their own vine and fig tree
And no one shall make them afraid
If we're to live up to our own time
Then victory won't lie in the blade
But in all the bridges we've made
That is the promise to glade
The hill we climb
If only we dare
It's because being American is more than a pride we
inherit,
it's the past we step into
and how we repair it
We've seen a force that would shatter our nation
rather than share it
Would destroy our country if it meant delaying
democracy
And this effort very nearly succeeded
But while democracy can be periodically delayed
it can never be permanently defeated

In this truth
in this faith we trust
For while we have our eyes on the future
history has its eyes on us
This is the era of just redemption
We feared at its inception
We did not feel prepared to be the heirs
of such a terrifying hour
but within it we found the power
to author a new chapter
To offer hope and laughter to ourselves
So while once we asked,
how could we possibly prevail over catastrophe?
Now we assert
How could catastrophe possibly prevail over us?
We will not march back to what was
but move to what shall be
A country that is bruised but whole,
benevolent but bold,
fierce and free
We will not be turned around
or interrupted by intimidation
because we know our inaction and inertia
will be the inheritance of the next generation
Our blunders become their burdens
But one thing is certain:
If we merge mercy with might,
and might with right,
then love becomes our legacy
and change our children's birthright
So let us leave behind a country
better than the one we were left with
Every breath from my bronze-pounded chest,
we will raise this wounded world into a wondrous one

We will rise from the gold-limbed hills of the west,
we will rise from the windswept northeast
where our forefathers first realized revolution
We will rise from the lake-rimmed cities of the
midwestern states,
we will rise from the sunbaked south
We will rebuild, reconcile and recover
and every known nook of our nation and
every corner called our country,
our people diverse and beautiful will emerge,
battered and beautiful
When day comes we step out of the shade,
aflame and unafraid
The new dawn blooms as we free it
For there is always light,
if only we're brave enough to see it
If only we're brave enough to be it."

There were two events, converging, that overwhelmed
me at that moment. First, I could not help but hear
Maya Angelou speaking through her. And remembering
that Maya, as a young child, experienced selective
mutism. Maya was sexually assaulted by a trusted adult
in her family. And when she told of the event, the
perpetrator was arrested. Shortly after his arrest he was
killed, most think at the hands of her uncles. After that
event Maya felt like her words had killed a man, so she
didn't have a voice for 5 years. And here was Amanda,
this young poet who, herself no stranger to a speech
impediment as a child (and as a young adult), sharing
such deep and profound wisdom. There's no way she
gained that much wisdom through observation in two
decades. Maya was there.

The second event that impacted me was watching Mike Pence. No longer a part of the inner circle, and mostly reviled by those around him, the Vice President seemed lonely on that podium. There is an initial pain and shock when one is discarded by a narcissist. Mr. Pence will have some work to do in the coming months. I hope he writes a book about it. Actually, I hope he smokes a bowl and chills out for a while and then writes a book about it.

Basil summed up my feelings pretty well: "Maybe, in his second life, he ends up being a good guy? Maybe he's had the black and white kicked out of him."

The phrase in the poem that got me was, "We will rise…" Followed by, "rebuild, reconcile, and recover." That's what Elko has been for me. A place to rebuild. I've got to tell you, there has been a fair bit of pain in that process. But it feels good. It feels like I am beginning to become acquainted with who I am. For the first time. And I feel like my time of selective mutism might be coming to a close. Maybe.

38.

During dinner one night Basil asked an interesting question, "Carl, have you ever seen a sign that says, 'Beware of Cat'?"

I can always count on Basil. "No, I can't say I have Basil. Only 'Beware of Dog' signs."

"Why is that?" Basil asked.

"Well, Basil, I guess it's because dogs have a history of being aggressive." I looked it up, and told Basil, "It looks like dogs kill 25,000 people a year! It looks like cats are responsible for zero human deaths. I guess there's your answer!"

"Where'd you get that statistic, Carl?" Basil asked.

I told him, "It's on the internet!"

Basil replied, "Melania Trump's tits are on the internet too, but that doesn't mean they're real!"

"Carl," Basil continued, "I'm disappointed in you. We've been friends for a while now. The headline reads that no cats have been caught killing humans. But 25,000 dogs have been caught killing? You really think that NO cats are murderers? NONE? Or maybe we just know how not to get caught?"

Basil thought for a minute then asked, "Hey Carl, you ever seen a 'Beware of Mosquito' sign?"

"No Basil," I said. "I don't believe I have."

"Odd," Basil said. "Mosquitos kill a million people a year."

"Where'd you hear that, Basil?" I asked.

Nothing. I'll try again.

"Basil? Where'd you get that info?"

"Sorry, Carl," Basil said. "You caught me daydreaming for a minute. Where were we?"

Never mind that, now I'm intrigued about Basil's daydream. So I asked him.

"Well, Carl," he began, "My daydreams fall into one of three categories. First, I daydream about food. Endless supplies of tuna. Second, the ladies get the silver medal. You let them take my balls, but they can't take soul! "Third, I daydream about switching places with you."

"Now that's interesting!" I said. "I get the first two, but tell me about the third."

Basil said, "Well, I don't want to be human. And if I were human I especially don't want to be you (a slight wink), but I wonder what I would do with autonomy. Probably safer for all of us that I don't have it. I like my life and I wouldn't really change it, but it's fun to play with sometimes."

"What would be the first thing you would do?" I asked him.

"Well," Basil pondered. "I guess I'd go shit in Jeffrey's mouth when he was sleeping and then kill me a bird."

I conceded, "Basil, there probably ought to be 'Beware of Cat' signs. Maybe even one on our front door!"

He smiled back at me, "You never know!"

39.

I woke up to my life today.

As you've been reading this maybe you've expected the story to resolve in a dream sequence, or maybe a coma. No. It's all been real. At least, this has been my reality. And I feel grateful today that the Universe, or God, or Mother Nature, or Bastet has seen fit to allow me the gift of Basil for a while.

He has been so many things for me here in Elko. A companion. A voice of reason. A priest. An accomplice. He has really been the best parts of the good parts I've left behind.

So when I woke up this morning, something was different. I woke up to my life. Not the life of someone's expectations. Not the life of someone's punishment. Not the life of greatness. Not the life of an ascetic. Nothing holy. Nothing carnal.

When I woke up, I was Carl. A dishwasher and generally a good guy. I woke up to my friend, Basil. Whose company and insight I value.

When I woke up I realized it was time to stop looking at the ground. Who I was doesn't exist anymore. Who I was isn't even real.

When I woke up today it was only today. Not yesterday. Not tomorrow. I felt the weight of only the present, which does carry some weight, but it felt light as a feather compared to what I was used to packing.

I woke up to the singular thought of breakfast. Not an existential dread within miles of me. My distant thought was about lunch. Dinner wasn't even a consideration.

As I'm sharing all of this with Basil over a bowl of cereal, he just sits back and listens, almost like he's admiring his own craftsmanship. He has worked hard on me over the past several months. I guess it has been a year now?

Basil asked, "So does this mean you might be a helper again?"

Tough question. I think I'm done helping for money. But I might need to be open to what crosses my path too.

Basil smiled and asked another question, "So, are you ready to ask Bumble out to dinner?"

I shot back, "Are you ready to have Jeffrey as a Step Brother?"

Basil didn't need to answer that one. His gaze and his silence were deafening.

40.

Last night I woke up in a bit of a panic. Another recurring nightmare, something that I have been unable to leave behind (fully). I don't have terrors anymore, but I guess I've still got some ghosts walking around in my subconscious.

I am in a grand hall, backstage wearing a tuxedo. I look out into the audience and I see a lot of familiar faces. But they are not there for entertainment. They have come for help. They are in pain. In the dream, their pain is soothed by music. And I am anxious to get to the piano on stage. I am eager for two reasons. First, I don't like to see people hurting. Second, I know I have caused some of the pain I see in the audience.

Curtain call.

I take my seat at the piano bench as the collective anticipation rises in the hall. We all know, instinctively, that the piano, not the person playing it, brings relief. But still, somebody has to play it. And tonight, that's me.

But as I raise my hands to the keyboard, I look down and I see my deformed hands. My fingers have been fused together and my hands resemble a mitten. I try to separate my fingers but they are not budging.

The crowd is anxious, stirring.

I lean into the microphone to try to ask for patience as I try to get my fingers unstuck. But I cannot speak. My mouth is missing.

The people are far enough away; they cannot see my panic. I try to leave the piano bench, but I look down and my feet are gone, my two legs are now one.

I cannot move. I can only watch the audience as their pain turns into anger. And I can do nothing about it.

I always wake from this dream in a start. No matter how many times I have this dream it always feels so real. You would think I could recognize it as a dream by now. But I can't. I startle awake, looking at my hands and feet, feeling my mouth. Relieved again.

But this night I did something different.

I said, "Hey Basil, are you awake?"

"I am now Carl!" Basil said with sleepy frustration.

I said, "Sorry, I didn't mean to wake you."

Still sleepy, Basil said, "I was just about to close the deal with Jessica Rabbit! What do you want?"

I didn't know what I wanted. So I didn't say anything. Basil broke the silence, "The piano dream again?"

"Yeah."

Basil said, "You haven't figured that one out yet?"

"Nope."

Basil asked, "Why do you think you are at the piano? You're not exactly skilled enough to fill a grand hall. So how did you get the gig?"

I'd never thought about that before, so I said the first thing that came to mind, "I guess I volunteered for it?"

Basil said, "That sounds like you. Offering to do things that are outside your scope. So if you don't belong on the stage, where do you think you belong?"

Another great question! "I guess in the audience?"

Basil asked, "You guess?"

"Yeah," I said. "In the audience."

Basil said, "Well, next time you have the dream, try sitting with everybody else. See who comes to the piano."

"Thanks, Basil. Goodnight. Tell Jessica 'Hi' for me!"

"I doubt she waited for me! Good night, Carl."

I have used my conscious state to impact dreams before, so the request wasn't so odd. I've been blessed and cursed with the ability to have lucid dreams. I journaled about it the next day and made a plan. I didn't have to wait long to try it out.

Two nights later I found myself in the familiar backstage place. Waiting for the cue to take my place at the piano. Instead, I just turned around and left the stage. I wound through the halls backstage until I found an entrance to the hall. I went in and sat down, just like I had rehearsed. This time I didn't recognize anyone in the hall, even though it was packed with people. This time, no one was in pain. There was nothing but joy and anticipation in the audience.

I waited a few minutes and then the curtain came up and a spotlight fell on the stage. I couldn't believe my eyes! What a glorious sight!

PART II

Basil goes on a
Road Trip

41.

I knew what it was as soon as I saw it taped to my door. I was immediately filled with a sense of panic and fear. I would have had an easier time tangling with a rattlesnake.

The notice said I had missed a piece of "certified mail." I'd like to meet the asshole that invented certified mail. The notice said I could pick it up at the post office in the morning. IN THE MORNING. I was muttering to myself when I walked in and I threw the notice on the counter.

Basil looked up at me from his self manicure, "Hey Carl, bad day at the office?"

"Basil, you know I don't have an office. I wash dishes. And no, I didn't have a bad day until I came home and found this notice on the door. Did you hear a knock?"

Basil said, "Yeah, he was here about 20 minutes before your got home. Since I still can't turn a doorknob I decided to ignore it. What is it?"

I told Basil what Certified Mail is. When someone wants to send you something IMPORTANT, and they want to make sure that you GOT IT. Because it's likely something you'd like to say you NEVER SAW. And when you miss the first delivery, you get to IMAGINE what might be in the envelope for the next 12 hours.

Basil said, "Damn Carl, maybe it's not bad news, did you ever think it might be some good news in that letter. Like, maybe you've been selected for free ass implants? Ever think of that?"

Basil's favorite hobby, distracting me with insults, is only mildly successful. He's right about one thing. I don't have an ass. I look like a frog standing up. But he's one to talk. Basil interrupts my train of thought with an out of tune rendition…

"I like big butts and I cannot lie…" He changed the chorus later in the song to, "Basil got back." Gotta admit, I was getting distracted.

I wondered most of the evening what it could be. I've received probably 20 pieces of certified mail in my life. None of it was good. At least I don't remember anything good. Mostly the parcels contained something along the lines of, "You did a bad thing. We know you did a bad thing. By signing this document, now we know that you know that we know." It's horseshit.

Basil and I spent the rest of the evening catching up on our shows. We usually like old re-runs, but lately we've been watching the Masked Singer. Not because I want to, but Basil is fascinated with it.

"Think about it, Carl. Close your eyes and listen to me for a minute. With your eyes closed I can make all the fucking sense in the world! Open your eyes and I'm a cat. Nobody listens to me. Only you!"

Basil and I ate dinner and watched our show. Well, I watched Basil watch his show, which is a show of its own. The only time I think about doing mushrooms is either watching this show or attending a cirque du soleil concert.

After the show, Basil was in the mood to sing a little, so he had me dial up some Elvis. Basil does a mean Elvis impersonation, minus the hips. I haven't asked, but I'd imagine a cat's hips don't rotate like that? Or it would lose something in the transition. I'm not sure. Anyway, Basil (unfortunately) chose to sing "Are You Lonesome Tonight." He does the song justice, it's just a hard one for me to hear. I've heard recordings of Elvis singing that song after Priscilla left him in 1972. It breaks my heart. You can hear it in his voice (and in his inability to finish even one live recording of that song after 1972). And it reminds me. I've had a true love. A One True Love. And I can't help thinking about her when I hear the song.

"Do you gaze at the doorstep and picture me there? Is your heart filled with pain, shall I come back again? Tell me dear, are you lonesome tonight?"

And then this line, "...you lied when you said you loved me."

I cry every time. Even when the damn cat is singing it.

Basil looks up at me and I know the look. He's deciding whether to be gentle with me or to break my balls. Tonight, he chose the latter.

"Dry it up, Margaret! For fuck's sake, she's a thousand miles away; years away from you! You think she's crying about you tonight? She's not; she's riding some guy she met at the bar! She's the queen of some double wide back home and she's guaranteed to have covered up that god awful tattoo of your name!"

Basil is not comfortable with emotion. He never has been. He hates talking about love and gratitude. When I'm sad it freaks him out; he doesn't know what to say. The only emotion he's comfortable with is anger. And after what he just said I'm angry. And he's happier that I am.

"Listen here you little fur ball piece of shit. You don't know what you're talking about! At least I've had a woman tattoo my name on her! You've got a smooth brain, you know that???"

Basil turned up a slight smile and his eyes twinkled, just barely, "My man."

42.

Having a vivid imagination isn't always a good thing. I tossed and turned all night trying to imagine what was waiting for me at the post office. By 3am I had pretty much concluded that the piece of certified mail was from a doctor I had seen several years ago and they just discovered a new form of cancer in my last blood sample. The good news: They were going to name the disease after me. The bad news: There's no cure.

I took the bus to the post office and waited impatiently in line. I can't tell you how thankful I am for social distancing. I say make it 12 feet.

Basil bet me the standard bet (a night of choosing what we watch on TV) I couldn't make it home before I opened the letter. We've been doing the standard bet for some time now, and when Basil wins it really is excruciating. He'll watch something he hates as long as he knows you hate it worse. The ruse is you can't leave the room and you can't sleep. One night we watched 3 hours of infomercials. I wanted to strangle him.

So I tucked the letter in my pocket and waited for the bus. What's another hour?

I came through the door and Basil was waiting for me with a premature grin of victory.

"Carl, get the popcorn ready, I've got a couple of good movies picked out for tonight!"

I pulled the envelope, unopened from my back pocket.

"Read it and weep you little hairball! Time for you to settle in for a Matlock Marathon!"

He couldn't believe it. He inspected the envelope for tampering, and then flipped me off with his polydactyl paw.

I couldn't wait any longer, so I tore open the envelope.

Dear Mr. Vincent,

Please accept our condolences as I regret to inform you that your mother, Jackie Vincent, is deceased. Her wishes included that you attend the reading of her Last Will and Testament to take place at 1:00pm on June 1, 2021 at Baltzer Law Group located at 187 N. Broadway, Lexington, KY.

Sincerely,

Amy Baltzer

Basil and I just sat and stared at each other for a minute. The silence wasn't awkward; both of us like to process for a bit. It was like my brain filled with every thought, every emotion, every memory from the last four decades. I was in desperate need of an air traffic controller for my mind. Finally, Basil broke the silence.

"So... road trip?"

"No, we're not going on a road trip!! I'm going to work and wash dishes. Then I'm coming home and we're eating dinner and watching Matlock and you'll just have to suffer through that. Then I'm going to bed and I'm getting up tomorrow and doing the same damn thing all over again. Road trip my ass! What? Did you think we were going to hop in a car that I don't own to go back East to a place I don't have to see people that aren't alive anymore? Or worse, to see people that don't care?? Oh, I know, we can go by to see my ex! See if she's still dining on little slivers of my soul!"

Basil just smiled at me. And he waited until I was finished.

"Carl, rant all you want. You know we're going. And I'm jacked to the tits about it! I've never been out of Elko and I can't wait to see where you came from! Let me know when you've worked out the details."

Do you know how infuriating it is to be so well known by a cat? He heard what I was saying, but we both knew I have to go. How to get there and whether to take Basil are matters I can sort out later. I can't imagine taking him and I can't imagine leaving him here. If I left him, he'd shit in my ear as soon as I fell asleep. If I took him, well, I'd have some explaining to do.

43.

I've told Basil my story, but it was my version. I'm sure he'd see things differently. Also, I haven't been back there (I almost said "home" but I'm home now) in quite a while. I have no idea what kind of reception I might get. Well, I do know the reception I'd get from some, and I'd rather not spend time and money to see that. But others, I'm not so sure. And how would I explain Basil? I'm a cat person all of a sudden? I mean I've always loved animals. But I wouldn't say I've ever been friends with one. And I've certainly never conversed with any. What if someone hears me talk to Basil?

And how am I supposed to get out there? I get by fine on my paycheck from the diner, but I also don't need much. I don't have a lot of walking around money. So a plane tick is out of the question. Greyhound has a "no animal" policy, unless its a service animal. I pitched the idea to Basil of him being my seeing eye cat. He shot that down before I could finish. Basil went on an extended rant about a company named Greyhound having a "no animal" policy ("The company is named after a fucking animal! Rosa Parks ain't got nothing on me. At least she got on the bus. I can't even get a seat!").

I don't have enough money to buy a car. Well, I could buy a car, but it wouldn't make the trip.

My last and only option was Amtrak. Elko does have a station, and I can get to Cincinnati for a couple of hundred bucks. Basil can ride in a carrier (he'll wish he'd picked the seeing eye cat). And I can get someone to drive up and get us. So I bought the tickets and told Basil we were, in fact, going on a road trip.

"I'm down! I've always wanted to see the part of the country that produced this fine specimen in front of me. Hey, do I get to meet your ex??"

"Basil, I can't imagine the comedy of errors that would allow you to do so. But if by some miracle you do get to meet her, you have to promise me here and now, you won't talk to me when she and I are together. That'd be too much for me. Just promise me you'll keep your trap shut."

"Carl, I'm sure I'll be struck dumb to be in the company of someone who voluntarily saw you naked. I won't say a word! Promise!"

"Basil, you're going with me on this trip for a couple of reasons. First, I could actually use the company. Strange as that is, it's true. Second, I'm not leaving you here alone. I'd get back and you'd be running a casino and a whorehouse out of the living room in no time. I can't risk it!"

"You know, that's not a bad idea! We could put a roulette table in the kitchen and a couple of blow up mattresses in the living room…call it Basil's Bets and Bareback Bitches!"

"Pack your bags, Basil. You're coming with me."

"What's to pack, Carl? You want me to put the litter box in the duffle bag?"

"Figure of speech, Basil. I just meant, 'plan on going.'"

"Kiss my ass, Carl. And that's a figure of speech. I'm going because I decided to go, not because you're 'allowing' me to go. Keeping you trained is making me exhausted! I need a drink!"

That's why I need him to go on this trip. He's the only one who can talk to me like that and I'll listen. And if I get in a bad spot, as much as I hate to admit it, I might need his hairy ass to get me out of a jam. As I'm thinking about it, I realize I need to make the trip as short as possible. Too many land mines back there. Too many zombies. Too much pain. Denial is really underrated as a coping skill.

44.

Prince Philip passed away. He was 99 years old. Married the queen in 1947. Basil and I watched the news together. Married for 74 years? To the Queen? Basil asked the question first.

"Do you think he was happy? I mean, he could have anything he wanted."

I had the same question. He never really looked happy to me. But then the only time I saw him was when a camera was stuck in his face. I wonder, in his last lucid moments, if he thought, "Well, that was awesome! That worked out better than I had hoped!" And if he didn't think that, then who could?

I wonder if mom thought that before she died? I wonder if she considered all of the years she devoted to chemicals and processes that took her away from her family?

I wonder what I'll think about, if I'm fortunate enough to have a moment with myself before I pass over? I remember in 2011 when I first heard about Bitcoin. It cost a dollar then. I thought about buying some. That year it soared up to $30 per coin and I kicked myself a little, but then it plummeted back down to two dollars (my memory might be a little shaky about that). I remember thinking, "Good thing I didn't sink any money into that!" Will I think about that while I'm about to pass over? Will I think about the people I loved or the people I hurt? Or the people who have passed before me? Or the people I hope not to meet on the other side. I know there's another side, but I have no idea what it's about. I can feel the separateness of my body and my energy. I never noticed that for decades. Maybe I started noticing the separation as my body has started a slight (very slight) decline in functioning. I feel a strengthening of my energy, so maybe there is where I notice the separation.

Basil interrupts my existential walkabout.

"Do you think he got laid a lot? I mean, it's not like the guy could walk around without a thousand cameras on him. So he almost had to be faithful by default. I guess my real question is, did he get as freaky as he wanted to? Or did he die with a ton of fantasies unfulfilled?"

"Basil, how would I know the answer to that? Did you get as freaky as you wanted?"

"Carl, you know that's a sensitive subject. I had my balls cut off before I could even talk. I'm counting on that nine lives shit and I'm going to be an absolute man whore for eight of them! I'm going to pull more tail than a special needs class at a petting zoo!"

"Basil, you can't say that. That's insensitive!"

"Carl, I'm a cat. Seriously. Go judge someone else."

45.

I was at work today and I let them know I was going to be taking a few days off. Bumble got a little worried about me, since she's never know me to take any time off. She has shared enough about her personal life that I felt a little obligated to give her some of the details. I told her about my mom passing and that my presence was requested at the reading of the will. I told her Basil and I were going to make the trip.

"Carl, you're taking Basil? That's cute! I'd be glad to make sure he's fed and watered if you want to leave him here."

That reminded me the last time someone offered to come by my place to "feed and water" Basil. I had to pull a double one day and Jeffrey asked if I wanted him to come by to "feed and water" Basil while I was gone. Basil was in the room and heard it.

"Feed and water??? You want to water me, Jeffrey?? Do I look like a fucking fern, Jeffrey?? Christ on a cracker, Carl, are you gonna let this wet lipped bone head talk about me that way??? Watered… I'll water him. I'd waterboard his pimply ass if I had opposable thumbs!"

Basil has a point. He's hopeful for a time when we get rid of the term, "Human Rights" and replace it with, "Living Rights." My relationship with Basil has made me wonder exactly how many living things are as sentient as he is. Like, I wonder if there's a cow or a chicken out there that has Basil's level of awareness. Given how much I like steak and eggs, I hope not. I'll just continue in my functional fiction that Basil is unique in that regard.

So Bumble's offer to "feed and water" Basil is graciously denied. But she's ever the curious one. She wanted to know if I had plans to see my ex when I went back East. First Basil and now Bumble! I've know for a while now that if I asked Bumble out on a date she'd probably accept. I also know she's not holding her breath. If there ever was a Carpe Diem girl, it's Bumble. She squeezes the most out of every day! But she has figured out that I'm not looking for romance these days. In her mind, my heart was broken by my ex back home and that's why I don't date out here. That's only partly right. The other part is, my life is pretty predictable these days. I like that. I generally don't have to wonder what's going on at home or what I'm going to walk in on at the end of the day. So both are true, really. I tried to answer her in a way that didn't invite any followup questions.

"I'm not planning on seeing anybody. Who I see, I see. I'll be back before you know it." But she didn't take the hint.

"C'mon Carl, don't you want to see how she's doing? Maybe she'd like to see you too?"

I was getting tired of the questions already. I'm sure my reply came off a little short.

"Bumble, when I feel like talking about it, you'd be one of the first ones I'd call."

She took the hint and winked at me when she walked away. She really is my type; a big heart with a messy past. But I'd rather take a cheese grater to my head than walk through those waters again. I'm certainly not taking this trip to "see how she's doing" or to rekindle anything. I brought everything I need with me to Elko. I'll be back soon enough to resume my peaceful life. That's the plan, anyway.

46.

My life in Elko has consists of home, grocery store, and the diner. Train trips and will readings are not on my regular schedule. I went to Goodwill and see if they had a Travel and Will Reading section. I'm not trying to impress anyone, but I also don't want to show up at the attorney's office in shorts and a t-shirt. I found a blazer and some pants that fit pretty well. I also found a couple of collared shirts. I took them home to try on and they seemed to fit. When I came out in the living room to show Basil his eyes got big and I saw the smile I'd come to dread a little. That smile means he's thinking, and that's usually not a good thing.

"Whoa! Carl! Save some pussy for the rest of us!!"

It's complicated. Basil has a way of making you the butt of his jokes, but they're also funny. So I'm pissed and suppressing a laugh at the same time. I knew he was just getting warmed up.

"You look like you're wearing a child sized trench coat. Did you join a cult that worships ponchos?"

I seriously don't know where he comes up with this shit. His brain just doesn't stop working. He ran through a couple of others that don't bear repeating, and then when the standup was over, he got quiet for a moment. I knew he was done poking fun.

"Seriously, it's not bad. Looks like some good travel and attorney attire. We can make it work."

Only a few more days until the new (new to me) clothes made it into a suitcase. Which I also got from Goodwill for $10. I had a suitcase when I got to Elko, but I was so certain I wasn't ever going to leave I traded it for an indoor antenna for the TV. Best trade I ever made.

That's when the knot in my stomach showed up. It had been so long since I felt it. Not nausea, maybe like pre-nausea? Like you know you're almost nauseous? I lived with that feeling so long that when it left me it felt strange for a while. I hadn't been in Elko for long, maybe a few days, and it just left me. I hadn't felt it since. Until now.

When you spend decades in a place it seems you collect a train of events and their corresponding emotions. At least I do. I don't have a quiet mind. My train isn't long or complicated here. Back home, it's a stretcher for sure. The Amtrak we're taking has about 10 cars; world record is about 80 cars. That's what going back reminds me of. A lot of cars behind an exhausted locomotive. The trip is going to be a lot like an Indiana Jones movie, except I don't look much like Harrison Ford, and the dangers we are avoiding are mostly emotional in nature. Mostly.

In spite of that I think it might be a good idea to drive past a couple of landmarks and show Basil a thing or two from my early years. The house I grew up in; the schools I went to; a few job sites. Maybe I'd like to see them too. But I'm already looking forward to getting back home; I know the Knot will be with me until I do.

47.

I didn't know my mom had a problem until I was a father myself. And even then, it took a few years after that. I did not grow up with an examined life. It was my only experience, and because I was busy doing other things, I didn't notice what was or wasn't maladaptive. Plus, I come from a family of secrets. We were taught to hide our flaws, and hide them well.

One of my best childhood memories was my mom and I walking from our house to the mall to go shopping. We only had one car at the time and dad needed it for work. So it was in the middle of the day and mom suggested we go pick out a toy. I couldn't believe my ears! Not only was she going to pay for it, but we were going to WALK there! I had the best mom on the planet! I got a cowboy action figure with guns and chaps and a hat. It wasn't Christmas or my birthday. Mom did some shopping too, and she got quite a few things.

My mom had a problem with excess. She always wanted more of whatever she was having, because more soothed her. But when more became a part of the whole, she wanted more still. This, I learned far too late in life, caused her all kinds of problems. More food causes obesity. More shopping causes financial hardships. More drugs causes dependence. All of her More's were costly, so I think my dad told her, if she wanted to continue getting More, she needed a Job to pay for it (there were, I later learned, some bad checks written for clothes she didn't need). So mom got a job, then another, then 10 more. Maybe 25 jobs that I remember? Working was not one of her More activities. She loved every job she went to. She sold clothes, she sat with federal prisoners, she taught music. She would come home from her first day ecstatic! She finally found her calling! Then, she'd get bored and quit within a week or two.

Dad worked at an Important Job with an Office and a Title. He was an engineer, and he was good at it. He was in charge of making machines, and then breaking them, and then figuring out how to make them so they wouldn't break that often. He understood his work very well. There are absolute rules in engineering. There is a finite tensile strength for all of the materials he used at his office. He was an Executive, but he also worked next to the manufacturing plant where they made the machines. I can smell it to this day. Oil and metal. Oil, metal, and math. That was his universe. Did he work a lot because he had to or wanted to? Who knows. But he knew the amount of force it took to break a piece of metal or plastic. He did not know how to measure the tensile strength of his wife or children. So mom and I were left to our own devices. She was broken, and she knew it. So was I, but I didn't know that yet. I just thought we were a lot alike. I wasn't wrong about that, either.

Maybe I'll take Basil by the old house, maybe take the walk to the mall. See what ghosts get conjured up along the way. This is the source of the Knot.

I'll take this trip, but I'll be glad when its over.

48.

Basil has only known Nevada, so to prepare for the trip he's been having Siri teach him about Kentucky while I'm at work. When I walked through the door the other night I was met with Basil's karaoke rendition of Achy Breaky Heart by Billy Ray Cyrus. Basil was leaned up against the coffee table with a blade of grass in the corner of his mouth as he sang, "But don't tell my heart, my achy, breaky heart, I just don't think he'd understand…" Basil paused the song and looked at he for a minute.

"Do I need a passport to go on this trip with you? Is there a crash course on the dialect I can take? And finally, does everybody date their sister in Kentucky?"

"Basil, I see you've grabbed all the low hanging fruit of that tree. Go ahead and get it out of your system. I'll wait."

"Well, if you're waiting, then… Do you know why there's no reverse cowgirl in Kentucky? Carl, do you know why?"

I answered him in my most bored voice. "No, Basil, why is there no reverse cowgirl in Kentucky?"

"You don't turn your back on family."

That's actually pretty funny, but I'm not telling him that. If I encourage it I'll have to listen to it all the way across the country. Still, pretty funny.

"Hey Carl, do you know what's similar between a tornado and a Kentucky divorce is? Either way, someone is losing a trailer!"

I gotta admit, he's picked some good material, but it's time for it to come to an end. "Hey Basil, you hear the one about the cat with 6 toes?"

"Dammit, Carl! Why do you have to shut me down like that? You know I'm just having a little fun. I only know one person from Kentucky and obviously I like him or I wouldn't keep him around. I promise, I'll leave all those jokes here! Serious question, though: How many people in your family resemble Billy Ray?"

"One, but we won't be seeing him."

"OK, last question for the night…"

"Promise??"

"Sort of… well, this is a two part question: First, did you ever have a mullet? Second, if you could show me a picture of that I'd appreciate it very much!"

"Basil, I may or may not have had a mullet at one point in my life. And no, there is no photographic proof."

"Did you ever go on a date with your cousin?"

"BASIL!!! ENOUGH!!!"

Thankfully, that ended it for the evening. Basil continued his self education about my home state. Eavesdropping a little, he actually seemed to want to learn a little about the place he'd be visiting. I never thought about it, but he might be a little nervous about the trip too.

49.

Basil asked me earlier today what happens when people die. He also asked what happens when animals die. He wanted to know if there was a difference, and if there was, why. I told him those were two very good questions, neither of which I had the answer to. He asked if I believed in Heaven. I told him I did.

"While you were at work the other day I heard someone talking about heaven on TV, so I did some research. Turns out there's a movie called, 'All Dogs Go To Heaven.' Which is a crock of shit. Then there's a song, 'If Heaven Ain't A Lot Like Dixie" by a guy named Hank. I looked up Dixie and, to sum it up, it's a pretty fucking racist place. So far, I've got barbarian dogs and racists up in that bitch. So, Carl, my question is, do we have an option or an alternative?"

Basil's not wrong. If I think about it, there's a lot of people (and more than a few dogs) who have claimed the destination of heaven. Many of whom I'd rather not be around. Basil went on to ask me why I believe in heaven. And what I thought it was like.

I didn't always believe in heaven. I guess it went like this: I didn't, then I did. Then I didn't. Then I wasn't sure. Then I became sure there was nothing after this life. Now I'm convinced there's a heaven and everybody gets to experience it. I didn't believe in heaven at first because nobody told me about it.

I grew up going to a Methodist church, but the only thing I remember about that was the shoes hurt and they all seemed angry about something. Then a neighbor boy and I were making ramps and riding bikes and he asked me, out of the blue, if I wanted to be saved. I asked why, and he said that's the only way to get to heaven when you die. I asked what I needed to do, and he said to just pray with him. So I did, right next to the outside air conditioner. It was the worst feeling I could remember to date. Worse than the church shoes, that's for sure.

A few years later and it seemed like I had to choose between titties and Jesus. I chose the titties. Heaven sounded like fun, but that was way in the future. My girlfriend had current titties and she didn't mind me playing with them.

So I didn't have much cognitive room for heaven. Later, when I worked for the church, I talked a lot about heaven, but I suspected it was out of reach. It didn't seem real to me. By then I started to see a lot of suffering, so I figured God took his ball and went home. Nothing but chaos out there.

Then an interesting thing happened. Two things, actually. I started having casual communion with God. Nothing formal. No buildings or pastors or liturgy. Just hanging out. Sharing space. Also, I started to sense something. This is going to sound strange, but you already know I talk to a cat, so fuck it. I started to sense a separation between my body and my spirit. As time and gravity have taken their toll, I have begun to notice a difference between my body and spirit. As much as I try to delay it, my body is slowing down. But my spirit continues to grow. The difference is more noticeable to me now. When I was 21 I couldn't even tell if I had a spirit, much less notice the difference. But I feel it now. My body can be sore and tired. At the same time, my spirit can be full of energy.

So that's how I described heaven to Basil. Heaven is an existence without friction. Totally fluid movement. No barriers. Not gravity or time or opposition or hate. Not trauma or illness or injury. No ego or pride.

Basil seemed to like my description. It was one of a handful of times he wasn't a smart ass. He followed up with this question: "So then your mom is in heaven right now?"

Of course she is. She's singing in the choir and writing bad checks and talking the heaven doctors into giving her fentanyl patches that she doesn't need. She is finally unrestricted.

So heaven is unrestricted existence. My mom certainly deserves that. Saddled with trauma and disease and maladaptive familial patterns her whole life. I didn't get what I needed from her, but in my final analysis, she simply didn't have it to give. And I've found some freedom in that alone.

50.

Basil looked down at dinner and said, "I expected nothing, and yet here I am...disappointed. Carl, seriously. Can you try something just a little creative for dinner? I swear, when it was raining brains you must have had an umbrella."

"Basil, you must think I'm the biggest idiot in the world, huh?"

"No Carl, you're not the biggest idiot in the world, but you better hope he doesn't die."

So Basil and I have this discussion from time to time. And when we do, I walk down to the grocery store and pick up some frozen fish. Which he devours. Which he, in turn, throws up. Which I clean up. And then he apologizes with, "I don't know what got into me." Just as sure as the Titanic sinks in the movie (spoiler), that's what's happening tonight.

The appetite is rarely connected to the memory. For some of us. For me and Basil, for sure.

51.

Packing Day. I'm a little nervy today, thinking about the trip. Thinking about taking Basil on a train. Thinking about dodging ghosts bask East. But at this point, what's the worst that could happen? I'm pretty sure I've seen the worst of it. Please, God, let that have been the worst of it.

Well, actually, when I mention "the worst of it" two things come to mind. First, when I realized she didn't love me anymore. That's the big one. It wasn't that I am unloveable (admittedly, hard to love, but it's possible), but she just ran out of love gas. She didn't have anything left in her tank. I felt as empty as a dishabited shell. It was ironic; my favorite times were when I made her happy. I loved seeing her contented. I'd love to know how she is now, but I don't dare inquire.

There's a phrase from my past that I remember, "Except when to do so would cause harm." It's from the Big Book and it references when it is OK to make amends, but the phrase applies to all kinds of situations. I'd love to see her, unless it would cause her harm. I'd really love to hold her if I'm being honest. But I'll not seek her out on this trip.

The second event that comes to mind was my first 72 hours in jail. The other 27 days were no picnic, but that first part nearly did me in. After a humiliating intake and medical assessment (a list of questions from a bored employee) I changed into my jumpsuit and followed the guard into a holding cell. I had been there about 3 hours at that time and it was late in the evening. The guard told me they were out of mats, and that I'd just have to find a spot to lay down until they found one. They didn't find one until the next day. The holding cell had about six "beds," which were rectangles of metal raised off the floor about a foot. There were about 15 people in the holding cell. Presumably, the first inmates got the "beds" and the rest of us got the floor. I was the last one in that night. My little piece of real estate was the last place on the floor that anybody wanted. Right next to the toilet. I had a mesh laundry bag that included a towel, a washcloth, and a thread bare blanket. Along with the clothes I brought in: underwear, socks, t-shirts, long johns. I used the mesh bag as a pillow and laid on the floor. For the next few hours I alternated between listening to strangers urinate next to my head and taking a full moral inventory about how I wound up there.

When I was in the fifth grade, in a new school, the teacher told the class, "Students, I'd like for you to break into groups of three. Make sure your group doesn't contain any of your friends." Instant panic for me. Even in grad school group projects caused me anxiety. Yet here I was sharing a very small space with people I didn't know. I don't stay at people's homes. I don't have sleepovers. The coldness of the floor and the proximity of strangers was only overshadowed by the megaphone in my head: "How did you end up here, you fucking idiot."

I have had what some catholics call the "dark night of the soul" before. In short, despair. There is a moment when someone leaps to their death from a tall place. That moment is between the leaping and the landing. That's what despair means to me. And that's what I felt. I didn't want to harm myself, but I also wouldn't have protested not waking up. My previous Dark Nights have been existential in nature. Feeling the chaos around me, doubting the existence or providence of God." But this night was literal. A literal hell. So many others have endured so much worse than that night. But I hadn't. Not in over five decades had I known a despair like that. I know I've just spoken about it, but I can't quite do it justice. To that end, it was unspeakable. Not for the shame of it. But because my vocabulary cannot depict it. And as I pack my clothes, I'd prefer not to be in the same region as that detention center. It was not a place of reform or restoration. It was, and this is the best description I can think of, a trauma factory.

52.

As the train lurched away from the station I couldn't help but remember how slowly I went to school as a kid versus how quickly I came home. It was almost like the train dreaded the trip. I looked down at Basil in his carrier under my seat. Since we didn't identify Basil as a service animal we had to split up our trip a bit. But I didn't mind. That just meant less time back East. Basil and I had the isle seat, an elderly gentleman named Walter had the window seat. The thousand dollar question was whether or not Walter was a talker. Such a coin toss on planes and trains! I was hoping for a weekend at Bernie's situation, but Walter seemed to be breathing.

Basil didn't care much for the carrier. "Why don't they put the humans in the carriers and let the cats free? There's no windows in this thing. No TV. No bathroom! Carl, what happens when I have to shit? Just go on the floor like a barbarian??"

I whispered, "Basil, I can't talk to you on this trip. If anybody hears me talking to a cat they'll lock me up for sure."

Basil was incredulous. "Oh, OK!! Lock up the feline and then pretend you don't know him! I see how it is! I thought we were going to be able to see the sights! This is horseshit, Carl!"

About that time Walter started talking. Turns out he sells vitamins. Well, he doesn't really sell vitamins, he tries to get other people to sell vitamins. And then, when he gets others to sign up to sell vitamins, they quickly transition into getting others to sell vitamins. I don't think an actual vitamin ever gets sold in the transaction. In fact, there may just be one actual vitamin and every new salesperson gets a picture of it.

Walter said, "Carl, would you say you're happy with your current financial situation?"

Basil said, "Holy shit, Carl! Of all the people we could be sitting with you picked the pyramid guy?? Did you see the girl across the isle and one row up? She's hot, and I bet she smells nice too! Why couldn't you sit with her??"

I didn't answer Basil. And I considered two answers for Walter:

"Walter, I'm completely happy with my current financial situation. In fact, Basil and I are just traveling on this train because we own a significant amount of stock in Amtrak and I'm looking for ways to increase our profits."

Or.

"Walter, can I call you Walter? Walter, I particularly enjoy the romantic company of older men. So if you are asking me out on a date, my answer is a resounding 'Yes!'"

I chose the second one, and Basil was losing it in his "cell." "My man! I couldn't have done it better myself! Well played!"

Walter turned away from me and didn't speak for the rest of the trip. I also decided we needed to rent a car at our next stop. I know exactly how Basil feels. Exactly.

53.

Basil and I got off the train at Salt Lake City and I rented an economy car for the remainder of the trip. Seeing Basil in the front seat of that little Chevy was worth the price.

"Carl, this is how you take a road trip! Want to take a detour? Just make the turn! Want to stop at a Stuckey's and get a pecan log? Take the exit!"

"Basil, how do you even know about Stuckey's? We don't have those out West."

"Siri, bitch."

I knew the answer before I asked. Basil loves telling me about his relationship with Siri. I came home one day from the diner and Basil was hysterically laughing on the floor. He couldn't wait for me to get home.

"Carl! Listen to this! You gotta hear this!! Hey Siri! Can you define 'mother' for me?"

Siri gave him a standard definition for the term, then Siri asked if he'd like more definitions.

Basil winked at me and said, "Yes!"

Siri continued, "Mother can be shorthand for motherfucker, a definition that counts as vulgar slang."

Basil was inconsolable. He had been trying to get Siri to cuss for the longest. Finally, he achieved it with the pinnacle of swear words. Well, maybe not the pinnacle, but pretty close to the top.

Basil was wiping tears away from his eyes. He looked like he had found a cure for heartworm. His joy was fairly short lived. Just days after he discovered this little easter egg, I guess somebody at Apple discovered it and promptly shut it down. Basil was distraught, but undaunted.

We stopped for gas and a few snacks. Basil, as it turns out, likes beef jerky. I let him nibble on some and then he got in the back seat to use the shit box I had in the floorboard. He doesn't like the car to be moving when he's in there. He says he's doing precision work (his words) and when the car is moving it throws off his rhythm.

That's when I saw the guy. The first thing I noticed was his walk. He walked with purpose, like he was going somewhere. He walked like he was on a mission. I imagined that people walked like that when they were on their way to the Oval Office. The second thing I noticed was his smile. He was full of joy and contentment. I can't remember seeing a person so happy. Eyes lit up, on an important voyage.

He wore shorts and a t-shirt, white tube socks and tennis shoes. He looked like he bathed every couple of days. He went over the 55 gallon trash can in front of the gas station and stuck his arm in up to the shoulder. I didn't expect that. He pulled his arm out and he had an aluminum can in his hand. He put that in a garbage bag and went fishing for more.

Have you ever actually looked in a gas station garbage can? He must have fished out a dozen cans out of it. When he was done, he wiped his face with the hand that had been doing the work and got a few old coffee grounds on his face. No matter. He's still smiling.

When he got his cans all organized in the bag, he took off the lid of the smoker's pole next to the trash can and fished out a couple of not quite smoked cigarette butts. He carefully returned the pole to its original position and, leaning up against the wall, lit one of the butts. His posture and face looked like a man who was resting after a satisfying day of work. A job well done.

By this time Basil had finished his business and was watching the guy with me from the front seat.

Basil said, "Would you look at that; an actual happy human! They ought to put him in a zoo!"

I asked him, "Why do you think he's so happy?"

Basil thought about it for a minute. "Well, the easy answer is that he's mentally challenged. At least that's what people think when they see him. The truth is probably more complicated than that. Actually, the guy reminds me of most cats. Most cats are that happy and contented."

I never really thought about it like that. Basil can be pretty grumpy when he wants to be. I pointed that out to him.

"Carl, in case you haven't figured it out yet, I like being grumpy sometimes. It's fun for me. I like to complain. If I'm complaining, it means that I'm smart enough to know the difference between what is and what should be. Yeah, I think that guy is happy because he knows that everything is going to be OK."

"Basil, you think everything is going to be OK???"

"Carl, I don't think it; I know it. Most cats, most animals, know it. The only time you see a neurotic animal is when they have a human around them that is neurotic. Except for rabies, we're all pretty chill creatures."

Basil and I sat in silence watching the can guy finish the last of his cigarette butt. He picked up his sack and walked briskly away, with a big smile on his face. Clearly, there were other garbage cans in the vicinity that needed his attention. I felt certain he would be back tomorrow if there ever was such a thing. But I don't think he thought much about tomorrow. Maybe Basil's right. Here I was thinking about this guy's tomorrow, and it probably never enters his mind.

My mentor calls this being mindful. I am thankful to have seen such a good example of it.

54.

To pass the time on the road Basil and I spent a few hours playing the Fortunate Game. In the game, someone starts a sentence, "Fortunately...." and then the next person has to use a sentence beginning with, "Unfortunately..." Here's an example: "Fortunately I learned to swim last summer." Then player 2 might say, "Unfortunately, I learned in the Nile River." Next player, "Fortunately, I am fluent in crocodile." You get the picture. Playing with Basil was pretty entertaining. I started things off:

"Fortunately, we're in a rental car instead of a train."
"Unfortunately, we're headed to Kentucky."
"Fortunately, we won't be there very long."
"Unfortunately, we will be there long enough for you to see your ex."

"Fortunately, my heart is closed for business and I will be unmoved by it."

"Unfortunately, your level of personal insight is just above that of a slug."

Basil broke the rules and kept going.

"And also, unfortunately, in addition to saying goodbye to your mother, you will soon see that your ex is the iceberg to your Titanic. Also unfortunately, you will be stunned back into the realization that she owns your heart."

Basil pisses me off regularly. But that little fucker knows me. And here's what he knows now. I'm a guy who lives in Nevada and who talks to a cat. The only creature I am willing to be vulnerable with is a furry feline. Basil knows that in order for this to be true I've had to encounter a love among loves and come out scathed. But there are no skin grafts for the damage that has been done. The scar tissue is a hard as Chinese algebra.

Fortunately, I'm over her. Unfortunately, that is the farthest thing from the truth.

55.

Following a long and comfortable silence (my favorite), Basil decided to settle an age old question.

"Carl, I'm really kind of tired of the debate between Dog people and Cat people. Can we just settle this right now? How many cats do you know who work for the cops? I'll just wait until you add up your number. Ever heard of a feline unit, Carl? Carl?? Snitches get stitches, Carl!"

56.

A tightness gripped my throat as we crossed into Kentucky. We still had a few hours to go, but I hadn't been in the State for quite a while. And when I left it, I left behind a lot of pain and more than a little failure.

The whole geographical cure thing, heading out West for a reset, was really a whole lot about the failure. If you break a piece of furniture, especially if its nice, you repair it. But there is a level of destruction that necessitates the item be given up to the dumpster. I felt like I had reached that critical mass. Nevada was, "can't fix it, gotta start from scratch."

Most people my age are settled now. Have been for decades. They have chosen a path and they've stuck to it. At least that's how it seems to me. I don't know a lot of people who are trying to sort things out when they're my age. Although, before I left, Roland and I were having a conversation (about what, I can't remember) and he said, "Guess what I just figured out about myself?" Roland is well past 75. I guess I'd rather be Roland, but this path (my destruction) has been tough. But Nevada, now that has been nice. Nice to not lug around so much regret and shame.

Three more hours and I'll be back at the scene of the crime. I almost wrote, "home." Home isn't where your heart is. Home is where you don't have to pretend. I'm driving across a State where I had to pretend to be a lot of things. So this isn't home. This is the opposite of home. Basil could feel the tension building in me, so he decided to try to lighten up the mood.

"A boob, a vagina, and an asshole are having a debate about who's best. The boob says she's admired the world around and provides nutrition. The vagina says she's the giver of life…"

Basil stopped there, so I asked, "So what'd the asshole say?"

Basil said, "Dunno Carl, we're waiting."

Basil started laughing so hard he coughed up a hairball. "Hey Carl! What'd the asshole say???"

"Basil, the asshole said there's 5 animal shelters between here and where we are going. I know how to travel light."

There was more comfortable silence after that, but Basil managed the occasional snicker under his breath. We filled the rest of the trip with a deep dive into Kentucky music. Basil was fascinated by the list I gave him as we went down the highway.

Basil knew about Chris Stapelton, but he'd not heard a lot of Tyler Childers. Basil loved Tyler's music, said he must have been a cat in another life. Quite a compliment. He also liked listening to old Exile cuts. Basil laughed at my story about dancing with JP Pennington one night when Exile was in Lexington. Basil said he bet I was a lot of fun when I used to drink. He's only partly wrong about that.

Basil liked Keith Whitley too, but said he could hear a pain in his voice that was unsettling.

Basil was also enthralled with John Jacob Niles and Lionel Hampton. Two pioneers that usually don't make the first cut of the conversation.

But the show stopper was Skeeter Davis. She was from Dry Ridge (I believe). Dolly and Tammy were influenced by Skeeter. I played Basil her most popular song, "The End of the World." Right as we were going through Bardstown.

Why does the sun go on shining?
Why does the sea rush to shore?
Don't they know it's the end of the world?
'Cause you don't love me any more

Why do the birds go on singing?
Why do the stars glow above?
Don't they know it's the end of the world?
It ended when I lost your love

I wake-up in the morning, and I wonder
Why everything's the same as it was
I can't understand, no, I can't understand
How life goes on the way it does

Why does my heart go on beating?
Why do these eyes of mine cry?
Don't they know it's the end of the world?
It ended when you said, "Good-bye"

Basil and I looked at each other, both with a little tear
in our eyes. Basil just said softly, "I get it."

I let that moment marinate just a little bit, then I
introduced Basil to My Morning Jacket. This was by far
his favorite Kentucky music group.

57.

How many versions of you are there? I know we all develop throughout our lifespan, but just from adulthood, think about your many iterations. As we drove into familiar ground I felt my Nevada self coming unzipped and being replaced by my Kentucky self. My Kentucky self is much more complicated than my Nevada self. That has to do somewhat with time, but also with intention.

That got me thinking about the purpose of our image. I have used my image, or my persona, to get romantic company, to get a job, to get a raise, to get out of trouble. To get into trouble. To manipulate. Cajole. Massage. In this state I have been a pastor, a counselor, and an inmate. If that's not complicated...

I decided to try an experiment. I decided to try to leave Nevada on and not put on Kentucky. Nevada is plain and uncomplicated. Nevada doesn't weigh the cost of the reply and Nevada doesn't much care about someone's response to the truth. So much less work than Kentucky. Kentucky is always measuring out the consequences of every response. Herding cats. A reference that Basil has always found puzzling.

So we'll try to keep Nevada on for the trip. What's the worst that can happen, really?

58.

Basil interrupted my train of thought, "So Carl, this ex of yours. Is she hot?"

"Basil, you know her name is Rose, and why are we talking about this??"

"Well, I just wanted to know what we're in for, that's all. I mean, if she's hot then I get to see you in the great internal battle. If she's busted up, I get to ride you about it on the way home. Speaking of riding, you rode her like a Christmas Pony, didn't you?"

"A Christmas Pony???"

"Now I've gotta explain my similes? Did you lose some IQ points as we've travelled East?

What I'm asking, Carl, is are you going to want to have sex with her when you see her or are you going to be glad you're not having sex with her anymore. Simple question."

"I'll want to have sex with her when I see her, but I WILL NOT have sex with her. She's moved on and so have I."

Basil just rolled his eyes at me. I guess I wasn't very convincing.

59.

It was late when we got into town. We didn't call anybody; nobody to call. So we just grabbed a room at a motel. The kind where the door opens up to the outside. Basil and I both liked the idea. The big chain hotels are kind of boring. Nothing ever happens there. I prefer a room and a show. The "show" at the motels I usually stay in starts around 11pm. This place was no different.

Even though it was $50 a night I still had to sneak Basil in. That really blows my mind. You can have a full on crack convention in one of these rooms, but you can't have a cat. Go figure.

We didn't exactly have a crack convention. It was more like a crack gathering. There was celebration and disappointment. Fights and sex. Transactions and robbery. You don't need a tv when you get one of these rooms. Just lay on the bed (above the comforter, please) and you'll have all the entertainment you could ask for.

Seems that Ray thought he should have gotten a longer (or better?) blowjob from Candy. I don't know how you value that particular service, but for $20 I would think Ray should just be happy she even looked at it. There were several arguments outside our room, all of which were both entertaining and sad. There really is no drug problem in America. Drugs are the result of the real problem. Don't ask me what that is, I'm not that smart. But the drugs are used to assuage the pain. Probably trauma. Experienced, complex, secondary, and transmitted trauma. But I'm no licensed clinician, so take that with a grain of salt.

60.

Basil and I sat in the lawyer's waiting room after a lengthy discussion as to why Basil needed to be there (he is, in fact, my emotional support). When I told the receptionist that my panic attacks included spontaneous diarrhea, she relented pretty quick. Basil was impressed with my new symptom.

"Spontaneous diarrhea??? Dude. That's like something I would come up with. I farted a little when you said that; maybe that contributed to her allowing me to stay. Man, you humans really think you're better than us. Technically, we're the indigenous species. By "we," of course, I mean "animals.""

"I think it was the comb jelly that was here first, and I don't think I'm related to the comb jelly. But I'm closer to the comb jelly than you are. Can you imagine what the first comb jelly thought? 'Man, this place is empty!" I hope he was an introvert. Well, I guess extroverts hadn't been invented yet…"

I could listen to his stream of consciousness for hours. He just says what comes up next in his mind, without filter or fear of being judged or demeaned. He makes a good case for doing away with clothes. We cover up a lot of bullshit with our clothes.

The lawyer came out to get us and frowned when she looked at Basil. Clearly a republican and not a fan of cats. Though the two aren't mutually exclusive.

Basil and I sat in her office. Wood paneling and a portrait of who I can only assume was the firm's founder. God, I hope it wasn't her husband. Mrs. Kerr was pretty starched. Rigid even. She didn't look like the kind of person who would enjoy a hot dog and a beer. She didn't look like she enjoyed much of anything. Based on facial expressions alone, I'd say the last time she had sex may be been during the Clinton administration. And then it was probably only missionary.

I had a question to start off the proceedings. "I know in the movies we see the reading of the will done as an event, but I also know that's not usually how it's done in real life. Why didn't I just receive a copy of the will in the mail? That would have been far less trouble, wouldn't it?"

She straightened her already straight back, "Well, Mr. Vincent, your mother was adamant that you be here in person. For what reason, I assure you, I don't know."

She glared at Basil when she said that last part.

Basil glared back and under his whiskers I heard him say, "Dusty bitch."

She handed a paper to me. Apparently, she had no intention of reading it; she would leave that up to me. So I read it aloud. For Basil, but it seemed to annoy her so that was nice.

I, Betty Vincent, being of full age and sound mind and memory, do make, publish and declare this to be my Last Will and Testament, hereby revoking and annulling any and all Last Will and Testaments or Codicils at any time heretofore made by me.

ITEM I
I direct that all my just debts, secured and unsecured, be paid as soon as reasonable after my death, provided, however, I direct that my Executor may cause any debt to be carried, renewed and refinanced for its repayment as my Executor may deem advisable taking into consideration the best interest of the beneficiaries hereunder.

ITEM II

All of the rest and residue of my property, real and personal, of every kind and description and whosoever situate, which I may own or have the right to dispose of at the time of my death, I give, devise, and bequeath to Carl and Rose Vincent.

ITEM III

I direct that my Executor and beneficiaries abide by any written statement or list by me directing the disposition of tangible personal property not specifically disposed of by this Last Will and Testament. This directive is mandatory to the extent allowed by law.

ITEM IV

The word "Executor" means the same as "Administrator", "Executrix", or "Personal Representative" and refers to the person who is to administer my estate and carry out the terms of this Last Will and Testament. I hereby name, constitute and appoint Carl Vincent as my Executor and direct that my Executor shall serve without bond. Signed, Betty Vincent. Witnessed by Rose Vincent.

Well, there it is. My mother and my ex have been in contact. In collusion, really. Now I see why my mom requested me to be here in person. The will necessitates that I have a conversation with Rose. Mom's estate doesn't amount to much, maybe a few thousand dollars after all her bills are paid (she was a very firm believer in "you can't take it with you").

Basil is eyeballing me. I can see it. I can feel it. He and my mom actually think a lot alike. This is a classic Basil move if there ever was one.

Basil asked me, "So when do I get to write my will?? I've got a few items I'd like to have in there. Your mom's a genius, really. You can't deny a person their last wish, especially after they're gone. Well played, Betty!"

There were instructions on what to do with her ashes (scatter them in in the Big Sandy). She said that river had tried to take her life on so many occasions it had the right to have her. She wanted several items donated to NAMI and her extensive wardrobe sent to the Women's Hope Center.

Basil and I left the lawyer's office without incident. Except Basil pissed in the elevator, but not because he had to.

We sat in the car in silence for a while as I processed the event. I had to call her. No two ways around it. I was pretty sure she wanted me to call her, but only to have another opportunity to tell me what a fuck up I was. Mom and Rose both wanted this meeting, but I thought for very different reasons. Mom always wanted Rose and I to work it out. I get that; those two were alike in so many ways. You can save your psychoanalysis of that if you don't mind. I've heard it all before.

There were some similarities between the two women. Both had big appetites for pleasure and big expectations for those around them. Both were given to bouts of depression. Both had the resilience of Goliath; surviving and even thriving after multiple and complex traumas. Both loved music and both loved to laugh. Both loved hard and strong. They also shared a temper.

Over the years, Mom had lost her bite as she aged. But that didn't stop her from sticking her lower jaw out in a menacing way when she didn't get what she wanted. It was cute in an elderly person. But in her prime, Mike Tyson would have gotten his ear bit off. Rose was not elderly, so her anger was, I suspected, in full regalia. She loved Game of Thrones (we both did), and she kind of identified with the Mother of Dragons. Really, somebody that's not to be fucked with. Rose was shown that way growing up. She modeled that way in her first marriage. She knew no other way. When she felt threatened, call in the dragons. They would lay waste to anything in their path. I knew that my upcoming conversation with Rose would include the dragons. I would rather do anything else in the whole wide world than see those fucking dragons again. It's not fear of the dragons that make me despise it so much. It's this: When she calls out the dragons I know how empty she feels. You can see it in her eyes. She is in deep pain, and she won't rest until you share it with her. In those moments she looks like the loneliest person on earth, and it hurts my soul to see that. Like I said, I'd rather do anything else than see that again.

Basil had a different perspective, "This is going to be worth the whole trip!"

Basil and I picked up mom and went back to the motel room. It was so surreal having the material that made up my mother contained in a small box. If you ever needed proof of an afterlife, this is it. Of course the box contained the materials that made up my mom. But it did not contain her. She was without borders, as we all are. The body just houses us. I'm staring at the proof. A box of material. This is only what housed her, but its all I can put my hands on, so it'll have to do. I wonder what she is doing right now? I wonder if she knows she is she? By the time I get my answer on that I won't be able to tell anyone.

Maybe I can tell a psychic. I recently read where a psychic had to cancel an engagement due to the pandemic. Pretty shitty psychic if you ask me. He should have known what was coming if he was any good at his job.

Basil broke my train of thought. "Carl, why do humans reduce their bodies to ashes and put them in a box?"

"I don't know, Basil. Some people do that, others choose to be buried in a box."

He had more questions, "So, there's a ceremony to it? You humans love your ceremonies. Birth, death, holidays. That's where we're different. When one of us dies, we notice it. But that's all. It's like, 'Hey, have you seen Bob?' 'Yeah, Bob got run over the other day.' 'Huh. Lucky bastard.' That's the extent of it. When you humans get buried in a box do you put clothes on the body?"

"Yeah, we put clothes on; nice ones. We fix their hair and do their makeup."

"Makeup??"

"Well, death isn't kind to the complexion."

"Wait, so people come by and look in the box???"

"Yeah, we call that 'visitation.'"

"What are you visiting??"

"Basil, I don't know, really."

"You humans are pretty fucked up! You put clothes and makeup on a dead body, then put them in the ground. Have you ever thought that, as a species, you all haven't reconciled with death at all?"

"Yeah, Basil, the thought occurs to me right now."

61.

Basil enjoyed the trip to the Eastern part of the state. There was a brief interruption when the news on the radio had a story about the Mayor of Chicago releasing feral cats to deal with the abundant rodent problem in the city. A shelter released 1,000 cats into the street to hunt and, as usual, Basil had a thought about that.

"Carl, do you think those cats will get hazard pay? Or any pay? They are performing a service for humans, right? When is it OK for a human to not pay for a service? Can they walk out of a restaurant without paying? Can they call a plumber and expect something for free?

Orkin would charge hundreds of thousands of dollars to combat that problem. Let the stray cats do it for free. They won't mind. Besides, it's free food for them! I'll tell you what, Carl, you guys are playing with fire. Assembling a thousand cats into forced labor isn't your best idea. All I'm saying, is when they organize you guys are fucked. Which do you think is easier? Catching, killing, and eating a hundred rats or one human?

They're feral but they're not stupid. We're not talking about dogs here, Carl. A thousand dogs couldn't find one tail. But a thousand cats? A thousand cats without manners? I'm no snitch, but I wouldn't plan a trip to Chicago if I were you."

After his rant, Basil calmed down and stared out the window for a bit. A few minutes later and he had another observation.

"Carl, where'd the middle class go?"

"What do you mean?"

"Well, I'm only seeing poverty or excess. Look at that house over there. That's gotta be worth a million dollars. We've passed several like it. But just a few miles back we saw a group of trailers that wouldn't sell at auction. Where's the middle class?"

Basil is nothing if not observant. He and I talked about the region and the struggles that have plagued the area for decades.

I told him about the opioid crisis and the impact it had to the region. I also told him about Big Pharma's role and how they referred to the residents of Eastern Kentucky as "pillbillies." That got to him.

"Fuckers. Whoever came up with that name needs to be injected with heroin daily for about a month and then cut off. Let's see how they handle it!"

"Damn, Basil, that's pretty harsh!"

"Nah, that's not harsh. Putting that pharma exec. in a room with a 400lb guy that hasn't showered in a month and then offering him a percocet for a sexual favor would be harsh. What's harsh, Carl, is your manners. Your "there's a right way to go about this" mentality has let a lot of people off the hook. I'd be a busy vigilante if I had opposable thumbs and reliable transportation."

62.

Basil and I (and mom) found ourselves on the banks of the Levisa Fork, a tributary of the Big Sandy. We were at the site of the 1958 bus crash. A school bus hit the back of a wrecker on US 23 and fell down an embankment into the Levisa Fork. The river was swollen with rains and snow thaw on that cold day in February. Twenty two children made it out of the bus onto the banks. Twenty six children and the bus driver perished. As news travelled about the wreck, frantic parents began to arrive on the scene to search for their child. They didn't know it then, but they had a little less than a 50% chance of finding their child alive.

My mother's father arrived in a panic looking for his daughter. He paced up and down the banks for hours looking for her until he received word that my mom didn't ride the bus that day. Strange to think about, but had my mom been on that bus that day I might not have had the chance to be here. Such an odd, unsettling thought; that my existence hung in the balance of such an insignificant choice. Also strange to think about what could have been for the 26 children that died that day.

Basil listened to the story in an unusually quiet way. Thoughtful even. It was very un-Basil like. I think he was realizing the importance of this moment for me. If Basil had any reverence in him, I was seeing it right now.

"Carl, I'm glad your mom didn't ride the bus that day. I'm also glad you are feeling overwhelmed by the chaos of it all. To feel anything else would just be due to ignorance."

A childhood memory assaulted me at that moment. I had not recalled it until right then. I was a child, maybe 10 years old. We had just brought my mom home from the hospital where she was receiving treatment for depression. I only know that now as an adult; then I was just told that mom had to be "away" for a while.
When she got home she was sad and tearful. My dad didn't know what to do with that. He never knew what to do with that, his brain just didn't work that way.

In that moment I felt responsible to care for my mom. And as I was sitting on her bed, holding her hand, she was repeating a phrase over and over, "I wish I was on that bus. I wish I was on that bus." I didn't learn about the bus crash until I was an adult, so I didn't understand what she was talking about. But I kept it to myself, sensing that the phrase would either hurt or confuse whoever heard it.

It is a lesson I am still unlearning. I try to make painful things not painful. For others. For myself. But pain can be a good short term teacher. Pain can point us in the direction of recovery. But there has always been value to me in removing pain. Let me rephrase that: I have considered myself valuable because of my ability to remove pain.

I cued up the Stanley Brothers single, "No School Bus in Heaven," not a big hit by any stretch, but one most folks around here have heard. Basil made a face but kept his mouth shut for once.

As I poured what remained of my mother into the stained water I had the strong sensation that she was finally free. Just like she wanted to be when the weight of her unquiet mind became too much. Just like she wanted to be when her process or chemical solutions failed to assuage the pain.

Just like she wanted to be when she had to endure countless acts of trauma and abuse growing up. And in that moment I found a space to love her more than I can ever recall.

Without the asterisk of blame or disappointment. In that moment I was able to navigate past the trauma and consequences of her choices. A tear welled up in my eye and I was only able to utter aloud one short phrase as I watched her ashes move away from me in the current: "What a beautiful woman."

63.

Basil and I spent the rest of the day touring the old haunts. I took him to Jenny Wiley park and showed him some beautiful scenery. We drove over to Prestonsburg and Allen and sat in front of a couple of houses that contained quite a few memories. We sat in front of a store that used to be Bennie's, a wooden floored general store where I used to get my orange pop if I was good. Just sitting in that vicinity I can smell that store. The floors, the summer heat, the sound of the cooler opening. All of the stores back home had a distinct smell along with uneven floors. I didn't know anybody's name in the stores back home when I was a kid. But Bennie knew me and I knew him. I felt important walking in there and being greeted by name. It wasn't a marketing strategy, but a math equation. Bennie didn't have that many customers. The Lexington stores had too many customers to remember names.

We drove by the "town" of David and the old farm. Parenthetical, because only a road sign is there to tell you where you were. I showed Basil where the old farm house used to be before it was consumed in the suspicious fire. We stopped and got out for a stretch and found ourselves at the banks of a small creek.

This was the site of my first loss. I had never experienced loss before what happened at this creek. I had a boat for my GI Joe and I had a string tied to it that was probably 25 feet long. I used to launch that boat and watch it move with the current and then retrieve it with the string. I used my chore money to buy the boat. One day the string broke and I watched in horror as the boat drifted out of sight, moving too fast for a boy to follow on the bank.

I felt loss for the first time. Something of value taken from me without warning. It wouldn't be the last time I felt that.

64.

As Basil and I drove back to Lexington I felt a deep sense of completion. Almost like the world was right, even though I knew it wasn't. I guess it was right in that moment. We use the phrase Rest In Peace when someone dies. The phrase is so overused that I don't often think of the meaning. But now, driving down the road, I felt like my mom finally knew peace, maybe for the first time in her life. The only times I ever saw her peaceful was when she was high or asleep. Or eating. A manufactured peace. Neurological reward is not peace, not by a long shot. But for some, my mom included, that's the best they can hope for on this earth.

Basil, as he is wont to do, shattered my thoughts once again, "Carl, does she have a nice ass?"

Had anybody else asked me that question I'd have been furious. But Basil wasn't being mean or crude, he just wanted to know if Rose had a nice ass or not. Simple question, really.

"Basil, it's world class."

"Nice! Do you think she still does? Asses change with time and gravity, you know."

"Basil, you can quit it now. I'm going to see her, and you're going to meet her. The three of us are meeting at a park tomorrow to catch up. You are invited on one condition: You have to act like a cat for the entire conversation. You can go back to being Basil after she leaves. But while we're all together, you're not saying anything beyond a 'meow,' got it?"

"Yeah, Carl. I got it. But if she's got a world class ass like you say, I might not be able to contain myself. But I'll try, I promise."

Somehow I'm not convinced. But I don't want to leave Basil for the meeting. I really want them both to meet. And as much as I don't want to admit it, what Basil thinks about her is important to me.

65.

Basil and I were posted up on a park bench a little early. I had a coffee for me, a saucer of cream for Basil, and my best recollection of her iced coffee drink that she used to like. I like gas station coffee the best, but she was always an expensive drink kind of girl. So when I ordered a Venti iced white mocha with sweet cream foam and extra caramel drizzle Basil looked over at me and muttered, "$8 for a coffee?? That ass better look like two cats fighting in a wool sock for that much trouble!"

Well, he's not wrong, once again.

I saw her before she saw me. That probably sums up our entire relationship. She got out of her car carrying a large cup from the place Basil and I just spent $8. So I just dumped mine in the trash can. No sense in looking stupid right off the bat. I'm sure I'll get there on my own.

She looked amazing, as usual. She smiled at me and I melted a little. We embraced briefly, awkwardly, and then I introduced Basil.

"Rose, this is Basil. Basil, meet Rose."

She smiled. You could tell she thought an introduction was a little over the top. But she didn't know Basil. Still, she reached down and stroked him behind his ear and said, "Basil, you're a cute thing, aren't you? Have you been keeping Carl out of trouble? Have you been keeping him away from those thirsty bitches out West?"

Basil looked at me and almost started to talk. I gave him the death stare so he just responded, "Meow" in the most forced way imaginable.

She smiled at me and said, "You're looking good. I guess the desert agrees with you?"

I blushed a little. "You look good too! How have you been?"

She ignored that question and answered the one I didn't ask. "Listen, I'm glad to see you and to catch up. Really, I am. But I don't have a serious talk in me right now. Not about us. So if you were planning on rehashing our past, I really can't right now, OK?"

"Sure," I said. "No worries. I just thought it was a good idea if we saw each other since I'm usually not back in this part of the country."

"Carl, I'm sorry about your mom. She was a beautiful woman! She made me feel more loved than my own mother. I'm sorry I didn't get to say goodbye to her."

"Yeah, she loved you too. You two had a lot in common."

She looked at me to see if that was a shitty comment or a compliment. When she saw that it was genuine, her face relaxed into a playful smile. I looked down at Basil and he was just pretending to be a cat. Lapping at the cream, doing cat things. But he was paying attention to every word and every look and every gesture.

When I looked back at her I found myself stunned by her beauty again. She always was a classic beauty. Tall, indigenous features. Beautiful skin. Transparent eyes, full of life. She looked better than when I left her. It looked like my absence had been good to her. And then I remember what Roland says, "It's not about you." Anyway, the time has been good to her.

Rarely is that true of any of us. Basil and I caught each other's eye and he could tell exactly what I was thinking. He was thinking the same thing: How did I end up with a woman as beautiful as this?

The silence was shattered with her next statement: "I got sober."

Basil muttered, "Holy shit! We'll never get back to Elko!"

I was stunned. I didn't know what to say. I had a million questions, but all I could eek out was a lame, "Hey, that's great!"

She said, "Yeah, not digging into it too much, but I thought you ought to know. I'm not doing the steps or anything, so you don't have to worry about an amends." She laughed at the non joke.

"So how long have you been sober?"

"About 9 months now. I switched therapists after you left and he gave me a new perspective. Decided it was time for a change."

I wanted to say a lot of things right then. I wanted to say how proud I was of her. I wanted to tell her to kiss my ass for waiting until I left. I wanted to ask if she was seeing anyone. I wanted to ask her if she was interested in seeing Nevada.

But I didn't ask any of those questions. It wasn't my place anymore. It's so weird when relationships go backwards. This woman who I used to share everything with, now she's someone I know.

So we kept it light. She caught me up on trivial things. I told her a few non-threatening stories about Nevada. Neither one of us was enjoying the chit chat. So she decided to take it a little deeper.

"So, are you seeing anyone?"

I looked at Basil. He was looking at me with daggers. I was going to get an earful as soon as we got in the car.

"No, I'm not seeing anyone."

This pleased her, although I'm not sure why. Her question almost required me to ask the same of her, but I didn't. She waited for me to though.

So many unsaid paragraphs going on between us led to some awkward silence, so we both stood up to say our goodbyes. We hugged a little longer this time and I made sure to take a deep breath to smell her one more time. I guess you can't really unknow a person; the embrace said what was unsaid.

I let go first, and she pulled back a little but didn't let go. Then she said it.

"You said you'd never stop loving me. You said it was forever."

A question hidden in the statement.

"Both are still true. Forever."

Our eyes were locked now, and I remember what it was like to be in her field of vision. I remember how nothing else mattered to me when she was looking at me. I didn't even feel the earth beneath my feet.

She smiled at my answer, "Good. Don't be a stranger, OK?"

She may be sober, but one thing was still the same. When she got what she wanted she was done. She didn't have any interest in telling me how she felt or if she was seeing anyone. I tried to kick the football again and she (just like Lucy) pulled it away at the last second.

That woman intoxicates me.

I felt numb (and aroused) watching her walk away. Basil hopped up on the bench and sat next to me.

"Did she say 'Don't be a stranger?' Seriously? Don't be a stranger?? Dude, that's kinda fucked up. Man, she had you. You were right. She's beautiful. But man, she had you. No wonder you moved to Elko!"

"Basil, she's always had me. That was never the problem. She never had room for me. That was the problem. I always thought it was the alcohol that was getting in the way. But she's sober now."

"Carl, you continue to reinforce my theory that you're a dumbass! Any idiot can see she is head over heels in love with you. Also, any moron, even at a casual glance, could tell she is only afraid of one thing: being weak. She's a strong woman, Carl. Independent. Not reliant on anybody. At least that's what she tells herself. That's her functional fiction. But love makes you weak. Love makes you bleed. Carl, she loves you. But she's not gonna love you on the outside. She has to protect herself. She's been hurt too many times. How can you not see that? Why do you think she drank in the first place?"

I was getting a little pissed. I don't want to hear it, especially not from Basil. But he kept on.

"When did she start drinking?"

"After her divorce from her first husband."

"Right. Because she fell in love with him. And he broke her heart. Didn't matter that he was a son of a bitch. She wasn't going to let anyone get that close again. Not even you."

I walked away at that point. I needed a minute. What Basil said makes sense, but I couldn't put it together how a cat who had never met her was able to discern that truth so quick. I guess I never accepted that truth because nobody wants to be runner up in love. Not much of a prize there.

I sat alone for an hour or so when I noticed the sun starting to set. I went back to the bench and Basil was taking a nap in the grass.

"Hey buddy, wake up. Time to head back to the hotel. We've got a long road ahead of us."

Basil stretched and yawned, "I'm your buddy now? OK, friendo, let's go get some supper and call it a night."

"Friendo? Basil, is that a movie reference?"

Basil grinned, "Maybe it is. Maybe it isn't. Either way, this is no country for old men."

66.

I don't feel old in Elko. I feel old here. Maybe it's the humidity. Probably it's the memories. Or the mountains of regret. My DNA is everywhere here. I've kept a light footprint in Elko. Maybe that is what makes me feel younger there. Either way, I'm ready to get back to where I belong. And I don't belong here.

67.

Basil and I packed up the car the next day and set off for home. No one to say goodbye to, so we just started down the highway. We chose a different route this time, just to add to the scenery. Basil is my best travel companion. Nothing forced. Nothing awkward. Just comfortable silence, good music, and nice mix of silly and serious conversation.

68.

Basil and I took a detour in Utah and spent a couple of days at Bryce Canyon National Park. It was wicked hot during the day, but the mornings and evenings were beautiful. He and I would check out the sunrise, pick a cool spot for the day, usually a creek or stream, and then venture back out for sunset. After sunset, as the darkness crept over the canyon, the stars came out in ways I had never seen before. Without light pollution, the sky lit up in magnificent ways. I told Basil I had a star named after Rose at one point.

He asked, "Which one?"

I knew it was a silly question. So I gave him a silly answer, "That one," and pointed toward the sky.

"Of course," he said. "I should have known! It looks just like her!"

"Not that one!" I feigned frustration. "Over there!"

Basil replied sarcastically, "I can't believe I missed it."

We both smiled at our own wittiness. The universe is so vast. And we are so small. The star doesn't know it was named after someone I love. I doubt she remembers there's a star named after her. Basil was on the same train of thought as I was.

"What'd they charge you for that? Naming the star?"

I thought about it for a minute. "Maybe $100? I think?"

Basil just chuckled. "Man, they saw you coming! Hey Carl, for $50 I'll let you name one of the testicles I used to have!"

The night was too beautiful to argue with him. Besides, he's right. I was just trying to show her she was important to me. It wasn't my best expenditure. Wasn't my worst, either.

Basil and I shared some more silence as we watched the night sky dance across the landscape. After a few more minutes of the light show, Basil took a deep breathe and whispered this little gem:

"Raised in chaos, stays in chaos."

I closed my eyes for a minute, just to let that marinate in my brain.

And when I looked over at him, he was gone. I assumed he stepped away to take care of business, but he didn't come back, so I got up to go looking for him. I spent an hour wandering around and calling his name. Several people heard me and asked if I had lost my dog. I got some pretty strange looks when I told them a cat I knew was missing. I didn't own him, after all. The word, "my," at least when it comes to animals, denotes ownership. Basil and I have already covered that concept.

After an hour of looking the truth finally dawned on me. Basil went away to die. He wanted to be alone for the end, so he must have wandered into the canyon. He and I had talked about dying before. Neither one of us wanted a witness to the event. So many people have talked about not wanting to be alone when they die. Or, you hear they died surrounded by those he loved. Fuck that. Basil and I both shared the belief that death was messy and ugly and transitional. A solo sport. I've been with people when they died. It's messy as hell. I'd cremate myself if I could when it was my time. Maybe I'll figure that out by then.

Even though I knew he wasn't coming back I still waited. I've been wrong enough times in my life that certainty has become a luxury I cannot afford.

As the sun rose the briskness of the night began to dissolve. With it so did my hope of finding Basil again. It is embarrassing to be a fully grown man wondering what I am to do without my partner, a talking cat. Even on days when he didn't talk, Basil was aware of my absence or presence. Therefore, I mattered. I was seen in the universe.

Who was going to laugh at my jokes? Who was going to get pissed at me for my idiosyncrasies? Who was I going to look after when I got home? Bumble? Jeffrey? Was the universe going to let me find another partner?

And then a wave of peace flooded me. I don't know how, and I'll never comprehend this fully, but in an instant I knew something that I didn't know before. Basil was not "gone." He wasn't in kitty heaven either. Basil was a being made of matter and that matter has only changed properties. I'm no scientist. I don't understand what I have written here.

It gets even more complicated, really. Not only do I know he is still "in tact," but (stay with me) he is now in me. A part of me. Not in a "I loved him so much that he'll always be a part of me" sentimental bullshit. I mean that in a literal way. He and I are now grafted. We are integrated, and there is no longer any difference between the two. And it seems that is what the universe was trying to achieve all along. That we were separated was unnatural. That we are now the same is how the universe wants it. How the fuck I came to this understanding I have no idea. But it's kicking my ass, that's for sure.

Now I know what to do. I have dishes to clean in Elko. It's time to go home. And on my way, and when I get there, I'll pay attention to the universe and see who I need to integrate into my life next.

I'm also wondering if the desert air would be good for Rose's allergies?

I suddenly have this strange craving for some tuna fish right about now. That's pretty different.

A serious note about giving up

I know what it is like to want to give up. All the way. But I wanted you to know something. I don't believe suicide is a sin and I think people ought to be able to make decisions about their own lives. I also think it is criminal to lock someone up for three days if they mention self-harm. I believe in agency.

That said, people that I know who have attempted suicide have communicated to me they don't think there's a way out. They don't see another option. I have felt lost before. I have felt like the road has run out. Nowhere to go. I have usually found these places because of choices I made, which compounds the desire to call it quits.

I guess I just wanted you to hear from me that what you might be going through is just a chapter. A dark, painful chapter. If that's the case, then don't put the book on you down before you're finished. Elko, Nevada is a real place with real people. There's thousands of places just like it.

I talked with a guy recently that was on the edge. He was angry. He was certain there was no way things were going to get better. He was lonely and misunderstood and broken. I've vacationed there myself. Several times. I've learned that nothing stays the same and nothing is as important as it feels in the moment. In fact, one could argue that nothing is really important, in the grand scheme.

I think about a friend of mine who is no longer on the earth. He left too soon for my taste. He's been gone for years, but one thing I remember about him is how much he loved his eggs in the morning. He and I would go to a place like the diner in Elko about once a week and have breakfast. He just loved his eggs. Over medium, mixed together, enough pepper to choke a grown man. Sopped up with toast at the end. Always with a great big smile on his face. I think about him frequently when I eat eggs. And I eat eggs every chance I get. Who knows when I won't be able to eat any more eggs?

It is your life, do what you want. But one of the great lessons I've learned is that my mistakes are temporary. If you need someone to talk to, the folks at the National Suicide Prevention Lifeline would like to chat with you: 800-273-8255.

The Other Saint Basil

Whether the character in this book is named after the spice or the person is up for debate. But I would be remiss in not acknowledging the original Saint Basil (330-379). He preferred the company of broken people.

Of his spiritual awakening he said:

"I had wasted much time on follies and spent nearly all my youth in vain labors…Suddenly, I awoke as out of a deep sleep…"

My man.

Made in the USA
Columbia, SC
04 September 2021

44861076R00141